Also by Tina Folsom

Samson's Lovely Mortal (Scanguards Vampires, Book 1)

Amaury's Hellion (Scanguards Vampires, Book 2)

Gabriel's Mate (Scanguards Vampires, Book 3)

Yvette's Haven (Scanguards Vampires, Book 4)

Zane's Redemption (Scanguards Vampires, Book 5)

A Touch of Greek (Out of Olympus, Book 1)

A Scent of Greek (Out of Olympus, Book 2)

Venice Vampyr - The Beginning (Novellas 1 - 3)

Lawful Escort

Tina Folsom

Acknowledgments

Many thanks to my critique partner Grace for her continued support, invaluable ideas, her laughter, and her friendship. And to my husband Mark for his patience, his love, and support.

A big THANK YOU to the readers and bloggers who help support my writing by spreading the word, recommending my books, and reviewing them.

ONE

Daniel Sinclair settled back into the comfortable leather seat of his limousine, which was taking him to JFK airport for his flight to San Francisco.

"We should be at the airport in forty-five minutes, sir," his driver Maurice announced.

"Thank you."

Instead of chartering his own jet as he often did when he traveled cross country, he'd decided to fly first class on a commercial airline. Since both his lead attorney and his girlfriend were scheduled to fly out to meet him on the West Coast the next day rather than joining him on this flight, there'd been no reason to charter a jet just for one passenger.

Audrey, his girlfriend of almost a year, had an important charity function to attend and had promised to take the first flight out the next morning, while his attorney Judd Baum was working on final contract revisions and thought it more prudent to finish them in New York where his staff could assist him.

Daniel had been working on the acquisition of the San Francisco-based financial services company for almost a year. Despite the fact that his attorneys and his business managers handled most of the details, he preferred to be intimately involved in any deal his company struck, especially when it came down to the final few days.

He always made a point of sitting at the table with the other side when the final signatures were exchanged, rather than finalizing the deal remotely. Besides, another trip to San Francisco would be just what he needed.

It provided him with an opportunity to relax as well as to catch up with his buddy Tim, who'd hightailed it out of New York five years earlier, having decided that life outside of California wasn't for him. The native Californian had tried to adjust to life on the East Coast, but deep down he'd never felt at home. Daniel couldn't really blame him.

Life in New York was hectic and completely centered around work.

His ulterior motive for coming to San Francisco, though, was to introduce Audrey to Tim, who had the uncanny ability to assess a person's character within five minutes. Things had been a bit on shaky ground with Audrey for the last few months, especially because he'd been working so damn hard on this deal.

Daniel had neglected her on several occasions and was wondering where to take the relationship. The truth was, he needed a little bit of advice from his old college buddy on what to do with her. He never discussed relationships or women with any of his friends or business associates in New York. Tim was the only person he felt comfortable with talking about other things than *guy stuff.*

He raked his long fingers through his dark hair, something he did frequently when he was preoccupied. His hair was longer than usual; lately, he hadn't even found time to visit his barber for a quick haircut. His schedule had been too hectic.

Never one to sit idly, Daniel opened his briefcase to start reviewing some of the documents for the deal. As he flipped through the files, he cursed under his breath. One of the files his assistant had put together for him was missing. He remembered that he'd taken it out of the briefcase the night before.

He'd gone to pick up Audrey from her apartment, but as usual she hadn't been ready, and he'd waited for her to get dressed. Since Audrey was never one to be rushed, he'd started reviewing the file while he'd waited for her and then promptly forgotten it there. And since he'd dropped her off after dinner rather than spending the night, he hadn't noticed his neglect.

As he thought about the previous evening, he had difficulty remembering when he'd last spent the night with her. It must have been more than a couple of weeks ago. And for that matter, it must have been a while since he'd had sex with her. Strangely enough, he hadn't even noticed. That's what work did to him—made him forget everything else.

"Maurice," he called out to his driver.

"Yes, Sir?"

"Swing by Miss Hawkins' place, please. I left some documents there last night."

"Certainly, Sir."

It wouldn't be much of a detour. Maurice was still fighting traffic in midtown, and Audrey's place was only a few blocks away. Daniel glanced at his watch. She was already at her charity event, but he had a key and could let himself in. The doorman knew him well and would have no objections to letting him go up.

Minutes later, Maurice double parked in front of the building, and Daniel sauntered out of the car. Audrey's apartment was on the top floor of the turn-of-the-century-co-op. He impatiently tapped his foot as the wood-paneled cab of the old-fashioned and rather slow elevator climbed from floor to floor.

There were only three units on the top floor, and he headed straight for Audrey's. As soon as he turned the key and let himself into the apartment, he thought he heard noises.

He wondered whether the housekeeper was there as he walked toward the bedroom, prepared to give Betty a fright. He liked the older woman, who always had a ready smile when he visited. She got a kick out of the occasional pranks he played on her, and she made him feel as if he were back in college.

Daniel listened. The sound was definitely coming from the bedroom. She probably had the TV on while she cleaned. Grinning and already imagining Betty's shocked face, he gripped the door handle, pushed it down slowly, and yanked the door open.

"Boo!" He almost chocked when he didn't see what he was expecting. This was definitely not Betty cleaning the apartment.

"Daniel!"

It was obvious that Audrey had decided not to go to the charity event after all. Naked, her hair a mess, her body sweaty and impaled on a naked male body, she'd never get ready in time. Not that she ever had any intention. Charity seemed to be furthest from her mind. The position she was in suggested anything but. Of course, Daniel could be mistaken.

Maybe Audrey was fucking his attorney out of charity.

"Judd. Audrey."

Audrey's long red hair cascaded over her breasts, strains of them sticking to her glistening skin. She'd obviously worked up some sweat riding him, and by the looks of the tangled sheets and the smell of sex in the air, this was a repeat session.

It also figured that Judd wasn't quite as busy with revisions to the contract as he'd claimed, otherwise, how would he have found the time to screw his boss' girlfriend? That he was screwing himself by doing that had obviously not yet crossed his mind. Maybe he wasn't quite as bright as Daniel had always thought.

Strangely, as he looked upon the scene before him, Daniel felt detached. And oddly relieved. Audrey's shocked face was the first genuine emotion he'd seen her exhibit in a long time.

"I can explain." Judd made a feeble attempt at disentangling himself from Audrey, who still straddled him even though she'd had the decency to stop moving up and down on Judd's cock, an action she would undoubtedly resume as soon as Daniel was gone.

Daniel lifted his hand. "Spare me." The situation was pretty self-explanatory from where he stood.

"Audrey, there's no need for you to fly out to California. Here's your key. We're done."

He placed her apartment key onto her dresser and picked up his file.

"Daniel, we need to talk about this."

He shook his head. He wasn't one to make a big scene. Hysterics were for women and gay guys. He'd never been emotional like others, at least not since puberty. Tim used to kid him, saying he didn't believe that Daniel's Italian mother was truly his mother, and he couldn't possibly be half Italian with the lack of emotion he showed.

At the door, Daniel turned once more. "And, Judd. You're fired. I'll finish the deal myself."

"But, you can't just fire me. You need me …"

Even though Judd had actually done him a favor by taking Audrey off his hands, he couldn't continue working with somebody, who went behind his back, especially not an attorney who he had to trust one hundred percent.

"You're replaceable. Get used to it." His stab at Judd wasn't referring to the job he'd just lost but to the woman in his arms. She'd replace him with somebody else soon enough. What an idiot.

Two minutes later, Daniel was leaving her building and was out of Audrey's life—for good. He felt as if his step was lighter when he walked toward the car, as if a burden had been lifted off his shoulders. He realized the loss of a good attorney hit him harder than the loss of Audrey. He definitely needed to replace him right now. Without a lawyer by his side to finish the acquisition, things could blow up in his face.

Daniel pulled out his cell phone and speed dialed as he got into the car, instructing his driver to continue to the airport.

The call was answered within two rings. "Tim, it's Daniel."

"Oh shit, did I screw up on your arrival time?" Tim was no scatterbrain, but after returning to California his social life had taken on massive proportions, and he was constantly hopping from one party to the next.

"No, 'course not. I'm still in New York." He heard Tim exhale, audibly relieved. "Listen, I need a favor. I need the best corporate legal firm out there to take over the deal."

"What, you ran out of attorneys in New York?"

"I fired Judd five minutes ago." He didn't feel like going into details. There'd be plenty of time to rehash the story when he got to San Francisco.

"Okay, I'm on it. I'll have somebody for you when you arrive. Can't wait to see you and finally meet Audrey. I made reservations for dinner. We can—"

Daniel interrupted him. "Yeah, about Audrey—"

"What about her?" Tim's voice was colored with more than just passing curiosity.

"She's not coming. It's over." He didn't even give his friend a chance to comment. "Which brings me to another issue. I have to attend that damn reception tomorrow night in anticipation of the acquisition. I was planning on having Audrey there to ward off those eligible bachelorettes they usually throw at me at those events, so I need a stand-in."

He wasn't interested in having to fend off advances of every woman under forty, who threw herself at him because he was rich and unmarried.

"A stand-in?" Tim's incredulous voice echoed through the cell phone.

Daniel ran his hand through his hair again, messing it up as if he'd just gotten out of bed, which couldn't be further from the truth. He'd been up since four in the morning to get in a workout in the gym before his busy day had started.

"Yes, some arm candy."

"I can set you up with a blind date," he suggested eagerly, obviously already having somebody in mind. "In fact, this is perfect timing. The roommate of a good friend of mine is—"

Daniel could virtually see Tim rub his hands together. "Forget it. I want a professional. No romantic entanglements, no blind dates." Yeah, that's what he needed like a hole in the head, a blind date.

"A professional?"

"Yes, what do they call them? Escorts." It had just come to him. That was the solution. Instead of a girlfriend, he needed an escort, somebody to indicate to all other women that he wasn't available. It would solve all his problems. And it would be way less hassle keeping an escort happy rather than a girlfriend or a date. Keeping an escort happy just meant paying her enough.

"Get me one of those. Not too pretty, just reasonable looking and with a bit of a brain so she doesn't embarrass me at the reception."

"You're kidding!" Even though he couldn't see Tim's face, he could tell that his friend's jaw had just dropped.

"I'm dead serious. So, make a booking for me. I assume they take credit cards?" If anything, Daniel was practical. That's why he was an excellent businessman.

"How the hell should I know? Do I look like someone who hangs out with escorts?" Tim sounded less miffed and more and more amused. Daniel could even hear what sounded like a stifled laugh coming through the phone.

"Come on, do this for me and I'll tell you why I broke up with Audrey." He knew just how much Tim liked some good gossip. In that respect gay men were like women.

"Every dirty detail?" he negotiated quickly.

"Can't get any dirtier than that."

"You're so on. Any preference? Brunette, blonde, redhead? Big boobs? Long legs?"

Daniel shook his head and grinned. It wasn't like he wanted to sleep with the escort; he just wanted her to accompany him to that darn reception. He really didn't care either way what she looked like, as long as she wasn't ugly and could parade as his girlfriend.

"Why don't you surprise me? See you soon." He was about to disconnect, then thought otherwise of it. "And, thanks Tim, for everything."

"Love you too."

How he'd ever ended up being best friends with a gay man, he had no idea. When he'd first invited Tim to his parents' house in the Hamptons during the summer holidays when they were attending college together, Daniel's parents had been afraid Daniel was about to tell them he was gay.

Just thinking back and remembering the relief on their faces when he'd told them that he was as straight as the A's he brought home from college, made him chuckle. Not that they wouldn't have loved him the same, they had assured him and given Tim an apologetic look, but they did want grandchildren one day. No pressure, of course. And yes, Tim was always welcome at their house.

They'd practically adopted him after that summer and, politically correct as they were, they loved parading him around, telling everybody who did or didn't want to know that Tim was gay and their straight son's best friend.

Daniel settled into his comfortable first class seat and reviewed the last remaining issues of the deal. He would have his assistant send all current contracts electronically to his new attorneys, who could take over where Judd had left off. At worst, it would delay the deal for a week, but he didn't care at this point.

Maybe he could use the downtime and go up to the wine country to relax for a few days. He'd ask Tim to recommend a place. As a wine snob, Tim was bound to know the best places in the area. He would unwind with a good bottle of wine in one hand and a book in the other.

Hell, who was he kidding? Since when did he know how to relax? During the last year, he hadn't taken a single day off away from his company. Even on Sundays, he'd been working, trying to put together another deal, even when Audrey had begged him to go away with her for a weekend. He couldn't really blame her that she'd found solace in Judd's arms. He hadn't exactly been the most attentive of boyfriends. Or the most romantic. He just wasn't the type.

Daniel already pitied the woman who fell for him one day. Good luck to her ever pulling him away from his work. Audrey certainly hadn't managed to, and she was beautiful and enticing. But his priority had always been his work, and that wouldn't change. Ever.

He hadn't come this far—and without taking any of his father's money—to have a woman stifle his ambition and make him feel guilty for not spending enough time with her. That was the path other men took. It wasn't his. He needed the challenge, the conquest, the battles. Not a woman sitting at home and whining that he didn't have time for her.

He'd pretty much given up on finding the right woman, suspecting that the woman who'd put up with him wasn't born yet. It wasn't that he hadn't tried, but the women he'd ended up attracting were like Audrey: high maintenance, spoiled, and ultimately after his money. No, thanks.

Looking back at his life, Daniel couldn't put his finger on the exact point when he'd turned from a fun loving young man into the driven businessman he was now. Women had always flocked to him, mostly because of his Italian good looks, so he'd never really had to work at it, and had taken them for granted.

Sex was certainly a part of his life, but not an important one. He'd often foregone sex with Audrey for late night business meetings. And it had seemed that she hadn't minded that much as long as he went to all-important society events with her. These events had been few and far between, as most of them bored the hell out of him.

Daniel rarely appeared in any gossip pages, which had bugged Audrey tremendously since she loved reading about herself in the papers. He was much more of a private person and certainly not as flashy as she'd wanted him to be. Looking back now, he didn't know why he'd ever started dating her. They were completely unsuited for each other.

Chapter Two

If only Sabrina Palmer had taken the other job she'd been offered and not this one at the Law Offices of Brand, Freeman & Merriweather, she wouldn't want to crawl out of her skin right now. She'd be sitting in an air conditioned law office in Stockton with a job that would probably go nowhere, rather than having one of the senior associates hover over her from behind, pretending to read the document on her computer screen when she knew he was peering down her blouse.

But no, Sabrina had to go for the job with the most reputable firm in San Francisco in the hope of gaining the right kind of legal experience to advance her career. She'd passed the bar with flying colors and thought she could take on the world, only to come up against an age-old problem: she was a woman in a man's world.

And now, instead of getting to work on any of the interesting cases the *male* junior associates were assigned to, she was relegated to routine corporate law while Jon Hannigan, or Slime Ball Jonny, as the secretaries called him behind his back, checked out her boobs.

Not that her boobs were that pronounced, but for her petite size she had a nicely proportioned set, together with a relatively curvy figure. Slim like a model she wasn't, nor was she tall. She would have loved to be at least a couple of inches taller so not all men would automatically be able to look down to her navel when she wore a vee neckline, but she couldn't change her genes.

Sabrina wore her hair shorter than she had in law school, and she'd recently had it trimmed so that it barely grazed her shoulders. It was what her enthusiastic hairstylist called darkest brown. He'd also begged her to allow him to lighten it up with highlights, but she'd refused each time and only let him layer it so it framed her face with a softer style.

"You'll need to rephrase this paragraph," Hannigan suggested as he leaned even closer and moved his arm past her shoulder to point at the screen. A whiff of body odor accompanied his movement. "You need to convey intent."

"I understand."

She knew all about intent. His intent. The day she was introduced to Jon Hannigan, she knew he'd be trouble. The sleazy look he'd given her had told her everything she needed to know: to be on guard. He'd squeezed her hand with his sausage fingers for far too long, and Sabrina had to keep all her cool not to yank it out from his grip, causing an unpleasant scene.

His pasty face was accentuated by an often slightly red nose, which could have been either caused by too much exposure to the sun or too much imbibing of alcohol. She suspected the latter. Hannigan wasn't handsome, but he wasn't particularly ugly either, even though this personality made him ugly from the inside.

If she had to describe him to anybody, she would have said he was average: just an average asshole.

"Sabrina, I'll let you in on a little secret. You want to move up here, you just stick with me."

Sabrina shuddered inwardly. Moving up wasn't what he had in mind, she was certain. Moving down was much more likely, down his body. She'd heard enough from the secretaries who'd been harassed by him. The mere recollection of what she'd heard made the hair on her neck stand up in high alert. The man was a pig.

"I can revise the brief first thing tomorrow. It'll be on your desk before you get in."

"How about *you*'ll be on my desk first thing in the morning?"

Sabrina sucked in a quick breath. Yes, she'd heard all right. Hannigan was getting more brazen. She had to get away, now.

"I'd better finish off for today," she said cautiously and powered down her computer.

Hannigan didn't make a move, but remained standing behind her chair, preventing her from pushing it back.

Turning her head slightly in his direction, she made another attempt. "Excuse me, please."

He moved back only a foot, enough for her to get out of her chair, but it brought her far too close to his body. She sucked in air and tried to squeeze past him. He had a sick grin pasted on his face. Did he really think he looked seductive like that? The homeless guy at the bus station had a better chance at getting into her pants than Hannigan.

"Why in such a hurry?"

"Doctor's appointment. Excuse me."

After giving her boobs another palpable glance, he moved aside and let her pass. Sabrina felt nauseous from the mix of his overwhelming cologne and his body odor. Without turning, she snatched her handbag off the desk and headed for the door.

"See you tomorrow, Sabrina."

His voice, too close behind her, made her speed up. She had to get out of there.

Even though it was barely four in the afternoon, and normally she worked at least past six o'clock, she couldn't stand it any longer. The doctor's appointment had been an excuse to escape Hannigan. Another minute in his presence and she would have puked or passed out.

How she was supposed to stick it out in this job for at least a full year, with him heavily breathing down her neck, or rather her blouse, she had no idea.

"Gone for the day?" Caroline, the receptionist asked as Sabrina passed through the foyer.

Sabrina answered with a look that said more than she could have imparted in a ten minute conversation.

"Hannigan again?"

She nodded and leaned over the counter to whisper to Caroline. "I don't know how much longer I can take this."

"You know what happened to Amy. If you complain, they'll just find a reason to get rid of you." The receptionist gave her a pitiful look. It was true. Apparently the partners valued Hannigan's achievements enough to overlook his indiscretions.

Old boys club, that's all it was. Like swimming against the current. The question was, how long was she going to struggle, or was she going to get out of the river?

"Doesn't leave me many options, does it? See you tomorrow."

Despite the fact that it was a warm summer day, Sabrina found the air refreshing when she stepped out of the building. She hadn't been able to breathe in her office at all, not with Hannigan around.

The funny thing was that the secretaries had been happy that the firm had finally hired a female junior associate. Now she knew why: Hannigan wasn't bothering the secretaries much anymore. Sabrina had become their lightning rod. As much as she felt for the secretaries, she had to look after herself and make a decision about what to do. Could she risk filing a formal complaint? How would this impact her career?

Remembering that the fridge at home was nearly empty, Sabrina decided to use the extra time to go grocery shopping on her way home. The supermarket was incredibly busy, and only one of the checkouts was staffed. Apparently some computer glitch had shut down all remaining checkouts.

While she made sure she could keep her place in line, she went back to the freezer aisle and picked up a pint of ice cream. She hoped Holly, her roommate and childhood friend, was home. Then they could devour Ben and Jerry's together while bitching about men in general and Hannigan in particular.

By the time Sabrina finally entered their shared flat, it was past six, the time she usually came home.

"Holly, you home?" she called out and headed for the kitchen, placing the bags of groceries onto the counter. Before the ice cream could melt, she put it in the freezer and turned when she heard a sound coming from the bathroom down the hall.

"Holly, you ok?"

The bathroom door was ajar. Holly was crouching on the floor in front of the toilet. She was in her pink bathrobe and throwing up.

"What's wrong, sweetie? Did you eat something bad?"

Sabrina squatted down and pulled her friend's long blonde hair back. Her face was ashen.

"Don't know. I was fine a couple of hours ago. But then ..."

Holly's head veered toward the porcelain throne again, and she lost yet more of the contents of her stomach. Sabrina rose and seized a washcloth from the linen closet, soaking it in cold water before she sat next to her friend again.

"Here you go, sweetie." She pressed the cold cloth against Holly's neck while she continued holding her friend's hair back. "Just get it all out."

"You look stressed. Bad day?" Holly tried to make conversation, evidently hoping to distract herself from her nausea.

Sabrina smiled gently. "Obviously not at bad as yours."

"Hannigan again?" Holly gave her a knowing look as she clutched her stomach again and held her head over the bowl.

"Not any worse than before," Sabrina lied. It *was* getting worse. He'd started making distinctly sexual suggestions and she'd run out of excuses to get out of his way. But she wasn't going to burden Holly with this right now.

"You should really do something about it." Holly was adamant.

"Well, let's take care of you first before we make any plans on how to deal with Hannigan, shall we?"

She helped Holly up and sensed how wobbly she was. Sabrina supported her weight while Holly cleaned her face and rinsed her mouth with mouthwash.

"Do you want to stretch out on the couch or your bed?"

"The couch, please."

While Sabrina helped her to the living room, the phone rang.

"Let the machine get it. I can imagine who that is."

Sabrina only raised her eyebrow, but didn't question her. Since she herself rarely ever got phone calls on their landline, she was pretty sure the call was for Holly anyway.

As soon as the beep sounded, an irritated female voice came through the answering machine. "Holly, it's Misty. I know you're there, so pick up the damn phone. Do you hear me? If you think you can just leave me a message to say you're not taking tonight's booking, you've got it coming. After what you did with the Japanese client last week, I have no more patience with you."

Sabrina sent her a questioning look, but Holly just scowled and shrugged.

"All the other girls are booked, so there's nobody to take your place. You'll work tonight, no matter how *sick* you are, or you won't work for me anymore. Do you hear me? And I'll make sure nobody else in town will hire you either. I hope we understand each other. I want you at the Mark Hopkins Intercontinental, Room 2307 tonight at 7pm, or you're fired."

The machine stopped.

"Old hag!" Holly croaked, her voice hoarse from throwing up.

"What was that with the Japanese client?" Sabrina looked at her friend, who made a telling hand movement.

"Pervert." At first it looked like Holly didn't want to give any more information, but Sabrina knew her friend well and knew that eventually she'd tell her what she wanted to know. Holly wasn't one to keep secrets.

"So, we're in his hotel room, and I think he just wants what most of these guys want. But no, that man had to go all kinky on me. He brought with him these little steel balls on a chain, and you really don't want to know what he wanted me to do with them ..."

Sabrina gave her a look, confirming that no details were necessary. She'd already received more information than she cared for.

"So, anyway, I bolted, and when Misty found out, she basically put me on probation. Said if I walked out on a client again, she'd fry my ass. Pardon my French."

Holly's French was never the problem. In fact, most of her clients liked her French and anything else she could do with her tongue. Sabrina shook her head and laughed.

"Let me make you some chamomile tea."

While she busied herself in the large eat-in kitchen and tried to find some dry crackers to go with the tea, Sabrina wondered whether any of her colleagues would find it strange that she shared a flat with a professional escort.

She and Holly had grown up together in a small town on the East Bay. They'd been best friends back then and had reconnected after college when they'd found out that they both had decided to move to San Francisco. Nothing had been more natural than sharing a flat.

While Sabrina went on to go to law school, Holly had bounced from one job to the next until she'd realized that there was an easier way to make money.

Blonde and blue-eyed, she was quite a beauty. In the right clothes, she was a stunner. So why go out on dates with guys, who'd just buy her dinner and then expected her to sleep with them, when she could actually get paid for what she was going to do anyway?

Of course, there were always clients like the Japanese businessman from the previous week, but according to Holly most of the guys were normal men, mostly businessmen from out of town feeling lonely.

At first, Sabrina had been shocked at Holly's choice to become an escort, but when she saw that Holly enjoyed her job, at least most of the time, and had remained the same kind of person, who she was before her odd career choice, she'd stopped trying to change her friend.

In any case, Holly's large income had come in handy when Sabrina hadn't been able to maintain her part-time waitress job during the last year of law school due to the demands of her studies. Holly had taken over paying the entire rent for the flat and always made sure the fridge was stocked.

Her friend had never let her pay anything back, not even now when Sabrina had gotten a job that paid her well enough to put a few hundred dollars aside every month. What were friends for, Holly had insisted. She was more a sister to her than a friend, and she knew Holly felt the same about her.

Holly was still as pale as Snow White when Sabrina brought her the tea and made her sip some of it. She was propped up on a couple of cushions.

"You can't possibly work tonight. She'll have to understand that."

Holly frowned. "That's what I told her, but you heard what she said. If I don't get my ass over there, I'm fired. And this time she means it."

Holly tried to sit up, but instantly dropped back into the cushions. "Oh, damn. So dizzy."

"You can't go. I'll call her and explain it." Sabrina got up but felt herself be pulled back by Holly's hand.

"You're not my mother, so don't. There's no use. She's about as understanding as Scrooge."

"Can't you find anybody to sub for you?" Surely there were other girls, who could take this call for her? There wasn't any convention in town at the moment, so business should be slow.

"I'm not a teacher, Sabrina, I'm an escort. We don't have a central system that we call when we need a substitute."

"There must be some *independents* out there. Don't you know anybody?" There was no way she'd let Holly work tonight. She needed her rest to recover from whatever bug she'd picked up. What if she had salmonella poisoning? No, she wouldn't let Holly exhaust herself today.

"What? You wanna do it?" Holly laughed and then stared at Sabrina's shocked face.

"Oh, come on, I wouldn't know what to do," Sabrina waved her off instantly. She and sex weren't exactly on speaking terms right now. She'd barely dated in years, and hadn't … Well, never mind. It wasn't an option. The closest she'd gotten to sex in the last three years was listening to Holly's stories about her clients.

"It would be perfect. Just look at it like a date."

"Out of the question." Was Holly completely out of her mind? She probably had a fever. Maybe Sabrina should get the thermometer and check. Or better yet, drive her to the hospital to make sure she wasn't delirious. She put a hand on Holly's forehead to feel if she was hot.

"What are you doing?"

"Checking if you're feverish."

"I'm not. Listen, you might not even have to sleep with him. Some of the guys just want company."

"Like they pay that kind of money just to talk to somebody, puh-lease!" Sabrina huffed indignantly. Not even *she* was that naïve. She knew exactly what an escort was expected to do, at least she knew enough from the stories Holly had told her. There was no need to find out first hand.

"And besides, I have enough trouble just fending off Hannigan every day."

"Well, that guy's a jerk," Holly commented. "I don't know why you haven't kicked him in the balls yet. I'll do it for you, if you let me." Holly's grin turned truly wicked. Sabrina knew her friend would thoroughly enjoy kicking the crap out of Hannigan. She knew all places where guys hurt the most—intimately. And she'd make full use of her knowledge.

"Maybe I'll let you do that one day. In the meantime, I still need my job." Sabrina tried not to think of the predicament she was in. She wanted her career to flourish, but she didn't want to do it at the expense of her integrity. Giving in to Hannigan would mean plum assignments to interesting cases, but nothing disgusted her more than the thought of Hannigan touching her. She'd rather have leeches put on her skin.

"And I need mine. We're in the same boat." Holly's voice sounded resigned.

Sabrina gave her a long look. What her friend was suggesting was too much of a stretch for her. "I can't. I can't just sleep with some guy I don't know."

Holly took her hand. "When did you last have sex?"

"You mean sex other than with a battery operated device made in China?"

"Yes, sex with a man."

"You know that as well as I do, so what's that got to do with anything?"

"When?" Even though Holly's voice was still weak, she wouldn't give up.

"First year of law school. As if you didn't know the story—hell, everybody watching YouTube sure had a good look at my ass." Sabrina shuddered at the memory of it. Without her knowledge, Brian had videotaped them having sex and then posted it on YouTube for everybody to see.

"That was quite unfortunate, I admit. However, you shouldn't let one bad experience like that hold you back. You need to let loose, pretend to be somebody else and just let yourself go. You can't wallow in those bad memories and be afraid of what the next guy is going to do. You've got to take charge of your life. If you assert yourself in your sex life, you'll get what you want. So, don't sit around like a wallflower. You're pretty, you're charming, you're smart. You could be anything. And you could get any guy you wanted."

Sabrina looked at her friend as if she'd lost her mind. She couldn't do what Holly suggested. "I could never pull it off." She could come up with a hundred reasons why she couldn't do it. "I'm not like you, Holly. I don't jump into bed with guys on the first date. Hell, I barely kiss on the first date. I'm *so* not a candidate for this."

"Bull! You took drama in college. Don't tell me you can't playact a little. Just pretend you're me. In fact, that's what you'll have to do anyway, so the whole thing doesn't blow up in your face, or in mine. You just go there and tell him you're Holly Foster, and then you'll behave like Holly Foster. Just pretend you're going on a blind date."

Strangely, the more Holly marketed the idea, the less unreasonable it sounded.

"A blind date? He'll buy me dinner, and then he'll expect to have sex with me. Like that?" Sabrina tried it on for size. It sounded strange in her ears. "Ridiculous. I'm not the type for this. You've known me all my life. What in my history makes you think I could even pull this off? The guy will see straight through me."

"Don't be so paranoid. All he'll see is your pretty face, and nothing else will matter. It'll be like a date, only that he paid for it in advance.

And you know exactly what's coming. In fact, you'll be in charge. Most guys let me take the lead. They want to be seduced. It'll give you some practice. I tell you, you sure need it."

That jab hurt. She'd put herself on the shelf after the disaster with her fellow student Brian, who'd obviously just wanted to see if he could get her into bed so he could post a sex video on the internet. The humiliation was something she never wanted to feel again.

She'd buried herself in her studies after that and rarely taken part in the school's social activities to avoid seeing him more than she had to.

"You need to get over it. What better way to do it, knowing exactly what you're up against? It's a one-night thing. He's from out of town. You'll never see him again. This is your chance to do something crazy, have fun, have fabulous sex, enjoy yourself, let loose."

Holly gingerly bit into a cracker as she glanced at Sabrina.

Sabrina was torn. She wanted to help her best friend out of a jam. Holly had helped her out so many times over the last few years, and she really owed her. But this? How could she agree to pretend to be an escort and go to a strange man's hotel room to have sex with him?

If her parents ever found out, they'd be appalled and sink into the ground out of shame for their daughter. Yet, one thing Holly had said, stuck. She *had* wallowed in her bad memories and hadn't let anybody close because of it. She was afraid of getting hurt again and had passed up sex because of it.

Perhaps it wasn't any worse than a blind date. Two strangers, a dinner, some sex. Wasn't that what most men expected anyway from the women they dated? Only they got away cheaper, with just a lousy dinner. Why not sell herself for something more, something closer to what she was actually worth?

And besides, she'd started missing sex and the touch of a man. You couldn't cuddle with a vibrator. But her fear of being hurt again had held her back from dating. She'd figured that once she met the right guy, things would fall into place. But they hadn't. She hadn't met anybody, and she was just as lonely now as she was after the debacle in law school.

Maybe Holly was right, and it was time to let loose and have one wild night with a stranger. Just one night. Without regret, without ever having to see the guy again, so there could be no embarrassment and no hurt. He wouldn't even know who she was. Anonymity was a great protector.

"Will I have to ask him for the money upfront?"

Holly smiled. "No. Everything's already paid for through the office. No messy dealings with cash. It'll be like a date."

Sabrina nodded slowly. There was no going back now. She had to be brave to help her friend—and herself in the process.

"Ok. I'll do it. I'll be Holly Foster for tonight."

Chapter Three

The minute Daniel opened the door to his hotel room, he realized why the escort agency had charged him an exorbitant amount of money for the pleasure of having the dark haired woman accompany him for the evening. She looked as if she'd stepped out of a fairy tale.

Her stunning green eyes looked at him. There was surprise in them as well as a silent question. Had she knocked on the wrong door? He hoped not.

If this was truly the escort they'd sent him, then he cursed himself already for not having asked more details about what he'd actually paid for. Was this strictly just a companion for the reception, or would she provide him with other, more personal services later?

Unable to speak, his eyes did all the talking for him, sweeping over the soft features of her face, her graceful neck and the slender curves accentuated by her light summer dress, short enough to show off her shapely legs all the way down to her elegant ankles. He noticed her chest rise with every breath she took.

Her breasts were a perfect size for his hands and firm without the aid of a bra. The slinky summer dress with spaghetti straps didn't allow for one.

How long he'd stared at her, Daniel truly couldn't tell. Maybe a second, or maybe as much as five minutes. But he knew why he was suddenly tongue-tied. It was a clear case of lust. Severe lust. Uncontrollable lust. Afraid he'd blurt out what was on his mind, something along the lines of *I want to fuck you now*, he clenched his jaw together and kept gazing at her lips. They were red and full and parting slightly as if waiting for his touch. He wished.

His imagination took him on a wild ride. He could see himself ripping the clothes off her body and ravishing her like a predator. Her soft body underneath his, he would ride her hard until she'd scream his name.

God, what he wanted her lips to do to him. Now. Instantly. He'd dated his fair share of pretty women and had bedded plenty of them, but the woman who stood before him was more than pretty. She looked like she was made for love.

And then she spoke. Like the soft trickle of a mountain spring, her voice pearled off her lips.

"I'm Holly, Holly Foster. The agency sent me." There was still some uncertainty in her eyes. She wasn't sure if she'd arrived at the correct room.

"Hi Holly, Holly Foster," he greeted her, letting her name roll off his tongue. "I'm Daniel, Daniel Sinclair."

She stretched out her hand, and he grasped it with his. "Hi Daniel, Daniel Sinclair," she repeated and chuckled nervously. The chuckle sliced right through his body, making him feel like a college boy again. Was she really his date for the night? When exactly had he died and gone to heaven? Had the plane crashed?

"Please, come in. I'll just get my jacket, and we can leave." Daniel motioned her into the suite. Damn reception. He could think of better things to do with her than drag her to a boring business event. Drag her to his bed was more like it.

**

As he disappeared in the adjoining bedroom, Sabrina took the time to calm her nerves. She'd passed the first hurdle. When he'd stared at her while she'd waited at the door, she'd not been sure if she'd come to the right room. Why would a man as gorgeous as Adonis need an escort?

His imposing figure clad in dark pants and a white dress shirt just reeked of breeding and confidence. Surely more than a dozen women on this hotel floor alone would have loved to run their hands through his thick dark hair and throw themselves at him—or under him. Why he needed to hire an escort when he could certainly get anything he wanted for free was beyond her.

Suddenly the thought of having sex with a stranger wasn't quite as daunting anymore. She'd do him anytime. God, she sounded like a hussy in her own mind. What had happened to the reserved and cautious woman she normally was? Had she turned into Holly already?

Sabrina was still absorbed in her thoughts when he returned from the bedroom, now wearing a matching jacket, making him look like he'd just stepped out of a fashion photo shoot. Why was a mortal allowed to look this good? Were the Gods messing with her?

"I'll fill you in on the way." Daniel took her arm and led her to the door. The feel of his hand on her naked skin sent warm tingles rippling through her body.

"Where are we going?"

"To a reception at the Fairmont."

As they made their way to the Fairmont Hotel, the famous hotel that had survived the 1906 earthquake, and which was located just across the street from the Mark Hopkins, he gave her more information.

"You'll be accompanying me to an important business reception. I'll introduce you as my girlfriend." He glanced at her and smiled. Walking next to him, she could smell his masculine scent. It was intoxicating.

"Will people believe that? Surely, they know whether or not you have a girlfriend." Her question about a potential girlfriend had nothing to do with the fact that she was skeptical about his plan. She was curious about the answer, which it seemed he didn't want to give.

"Don't worry. Nobody knows anything about my private life. They're all business acquaintances. So, here's your job for tonight: stay by my side, flirt with me, and if we do get separated and you see me talking to any woman under forty, rescue me."

"Rescue you?" Sabrina gave him a surprised look from the side. God, his profile was stunning.

Daniel laughed softly. "Yes, and that's your most important job for tonight. I don't want any of these eligible single women digging their claws into me thinking they can … Well, anyway, if any of them come too close, you need to jump in and assert your claim on me. Make sure they know you mean business."

Sabrina laughed. "Any preference on how I should assert my claim?" She had a few ideas herself but didn't want to be presumptuous.

The look Daniel gave her was searing hot, unless she'd completely lost her mind and projected onto him what she wanted to see. "An intimate touch always works wonders, trust me. And any appropriate terms of endearment will be appreciated too."

"I'm sure I can come up with something."

His eyes locked with hers. "I'm positive you can."

At the door to the hall where the reception was being held at, they stopped. "I should hold your hand when we go in there."

She swallowed hard. "Of course."

When he took her hand and intertwined his fingers with hers, a bolt of lightning shot through her body. She was surprised at herself. Never had a simple touch by a man had such a profound effect on her.

The hall was busy. Sabrina estimated that over a hundred well-dressed people were in attendance. Waiters circulated with platters of canapés and trays of champagne. While there were certainly many women in attendance, there was an overwhelming number of men dressed in dark suits, some looking more bored than others. Lawyers, for sure. She recognized the type.

Daniel pulled her with him as they made their way through the crowd to the back of the room. He gave off an air of confidence and determination, as if this were his backyard.

"Ah, there you are. We were wondering when you'd show." A distinguished gentleman in his late fifties stopped them.

"Martin. Nice to see you again." Daniel stretched out his hand and shook Martin's.

"May I introduce my wife? Nancy, this is Daniel Sinclair, the man who's buying us out."

The petite woman on Martin's arm smiled broadly and shook Daniel's outstretched hand. "Such a pleasure to finally meet you," she chirped while she glanced at Sabrina.

"Likewise. I suppose you'll see much more of Martin once this deal is finalized."

Nancy nudged her husband in the ribs and rolled her eyes. "Don't remind me. He's going to drive me crazy spending so much time at home."

Her husband returned a loving smile. "She's just joking. In reality, she can't wait to have me spend more time with her. But enough about us." Martin's eyes rested on Sabrina. "Daniel, would you introduce us to your companion?"

"My apologies. Martin, Nancy, this is Holly, my fiancée."

As soon as the words were out of Daniel's mouth, Sabrina gave him a surprised look but immediately turned back to their hosts and flashed them a charming smile. Why hadn't he stuck to his original plan? Why suddenly upgrade her to fiancée?

After exchanging handshakes and greetings, they started to make small talk.

"You don't sound like you're from New York, Holly," Nancy remarked.

"I'm not. I'm from the Bay Area."

Martin gave Daniel a knowing look. "I see. So my company isn't the only *acquisition* you're making in San Francisco."

Daniel grinned and led Sabrina's hand to his mouth, planting a small kiss on it. "Guilty as charged."

The kiss was unexpected and made Sabrina's heart beat faster. She smiled at him briefly, but the kiss hadn't affected him at all. It seemed he was used to pretend things that weren't true.

"What do you do, Holly?" Nancy asked.

***

When Daniel heard Nancy's question, he flinched. Damn, they hadn't discussed a back story at all. He glanced at Holly trying to catch her eye, wondering whether she could improvise, but her mouth was already in motion.

"I'm an attorney," she offered. He blinked his eyes shut for a second as if waiting for a bomb to drop. Hell, she'd trip herself up with a statement like that. There were more lawyers in the hall than at a legal convention in Las Vegas. He should have briefed her before their arrival. This was a disaster waiting to happen.

"Let's not talk business, shall we?" he cut in, trying to save the day. "Champagne, darling?" He stopped a waiter and took two glasses off the tray, handing her one. Too late: Nancy had already waved a man to them. Daniel recognized him. He was one of the attorneys working on the acquisition.

"Bob, you know Daniel already, but let me introduce his fiancée to you, Holly Foster. She's an attorney."

Shit. Daniel almost choked on his champagne. How would his pretty escort handle this? Bob was never one for small talk. All this lanky attorney ever talked about was his work.

"Nice to meet you, Holly. Which school?" As Daniel had predicted, Bob went right down to business.

"Hastings," she replied without hesitation.

"Wow, what a coincidence. Class of '99. Is Bunburry still teaching?" Bob was in his element. Perfect, the whole charade would blow up in his face in the next two minutes, Daniel was sure. Couldn't she at least have chosen some obscure little school somewhere out in the boonies, rather than Hastings School of Law, which even he as an out-of-towner knew, was right in San Francisco? She probably didn't know of any other law school. Figured. God, he was so screwed.

"He retired last year, finally," Sabrina answered confidently.

Bob nodded understandingly. "About time." Lucky guess, Daniel reckoned.

Before he could disrupt the conversation and steer it in another direction, Martin interrupted him to introduce a beautiful redhead.

"You have to meet Grace Anderson. She sits on practically every charity board in the city. Grace, dear, this is Daniel Sinclair."

Grace blew a kiss into Martin's direction and immediately locked onto Daniel. He'd seen that look before. He was being sized up by a woman who knew what she was looking for: a wealthy husband. Glancing back, he saw that his pretend fiancée was in deep conversation with Bob. Bad timing.

"Nice to meet you, Ms Anderson."

Daniel shook her hand and let go of it as soon as he could.

"Why so formal? Please call me Grace." Her saccharine sweet smile was nauseating. This was exactly what he'd been trying to avoid. He felt like a caged tiger, just a little less tame. Her suggestive smile told him unmistakably that she was going to make a move on him as soon as he let his guard down.

"Which charities are you involved it?" He had to make small talk, even though he had no interest in talking to this woman at all. She was a carbon copy of Audrey: shallow, pretentious, and out to find a rich husband. Funny, how now that he'd broken up with Audrey, he could see her for what she truly was.

Daniel barely listened to the woman's chatter and instead tried to hone in on the conversation between Holly and Bob, but they were too far away for him to pick up any snippets over the din of voices in the hall.

He realized that Grace had stopped talking and asked him something, when he suddenly felt her hand on his forearm.

"Don't you think so?"

He gave a non-committal smile and wondered how he could get out of her clutches.

"Darling," a voice from behind saved him. He turned gratefully as he felt Holly's hand on his back. "Bob was just telling me the funniest story about his law school days. I think you'll get a kick out of it, especially since you love baseball." Sabrina gave Grace a pointed look, then lowered her eyes to where her hand rested on his arm. "Excuse us. I'll have to steal my fiancé for a moment."

Grace instantly withdrew her hand as if she'd been burned.

Sabrina pulled him away out of earshot of the woman. "Was that all right?"

Daniel took a step closer to her. "Perfect," he said and planted a quick kiss on her cheek—her now flushed cheek. "That was close. I don't know how these women hone in on bachelors within seconds. She was about to dig her claws into me."

"One of her claws was already on you." Holly chuckled softly. "You don't like women much, huh?"

He gave her an astonished look. "No, that's not it. I don't like gold diggers much. So, how did you manage to survive Bob?"

"Easy. Don't worry about me. I can handle Bob."

He gave her an admiring glance. She evidently could handle Bob. He figured there were a lot of other things she could handle too, maybe even him. Maybe he could get a taste tonight of exactly *how* she would handle him.

"Come, we'll have to mingle a little before we can get out of this circus." He took her hand again, not that it was necessary, but he wanted to. He liked touching her.

***

Sabrina enjoyed the evening. Daniel introduced her to many people, whose names she instantly forgot as they moved on to others, who wanted to make her acquaintance.

From all the chitchat, she'd pieced together that Daniel was in town to finalize the acquisition of a company, and given the many beautiful young women, who wanted to meet him, she also realized that he was one of the most eligible bachelors currently in town. No wonder he wanted somebody as a buffer. She did her best to scare all women away as he'd requested.

Even though it was her job for the evening, she loved it. She loved touching him, taking his hand, calling him darling. He'd kissed her on the cheek only that one time, and she wondered whether he'd do it again. His lips had felt so warm and tender, she'd started fantasizing about how his lips would feel on other parts of her body. The thought made her feel flushed.

Since he'd obviously simply hired her to be his pretend girlfriend, though inexplicably elevated her to fiancée status, in order to ward off other women, there was little chance he actually wanted to have sex with her. He seemed like a man who chose his sexual partners carefully and not like one who'd hop into bed with an escort, not even a pretend escort.

Well, at least she got a nice evening out with a charming and attentive man. The envious glances many of the young women gave her throughout the evening confirmed that she wasn't the only one who thought Daniel was yummy.

Strangely enough, he didn't seem to like the attention those women paid him. Most of his conversations were held with some of the men in the room and centered on business. Whenever he was introduced to a woman, especially an unattached one, he extracted himself from the conversation as quickly as possible.

Most times he used her as an excuse.

"Holly, darling, can I get you another drink?" he said smilingly as another young woman tried to drag him into a conversation. Sabrina stretched out to hand him her empty glass and while he took it out of her hand and put it onto a side table, he led her hand to his mouth, kissing her fingertips in full view of the other woman who instantly made her exit.

"You're terrible," Sabrina chastised him laughingly, knowing he'd deliberately showed affection in order to get rid of the other woman.

"I can't help myself." Daniel winked at her. Whatever he meant by that, she wasn't going to ask.

"Ever heard of self-control?" she teased.

"Impossible to achieve in the presence of a beautiful woman."

"Which one?" Sabrina let her gaze wander around the room.

He didn't answer and instead pulled her with him to make more introductions.

Later, she and Daniel stood next to a beautiful arrangement of colorful flowers at one end of the large hall. As a waiter passed by, Sabrina snatched another canapé off the tray and devoured it. She'd stopped counting how many delicious little canapés she'd already scarfed down and didn't care. What did it matter if she gained another pound? It wasn't like anybody would see her naked anytime soon.

Daniel smiled at her briefly and continued his conversation with Martin while his wife carried on telling her what travels she and her husband had planned after the deal was done.

Sabrina listened politely and asked questions whenever the opportunity arose until suddenly her nose started twitching uncomfortably. She tried to hold back a sneeze, but too late. Her sneeze was too loud for polite society, she was sure.

"Bless you!" all three of them said in unison.

"Allergies," Sabrina replied apologetically and pointed at the flowers while she rummaged in her small handbag to find her handkerchief. She never left home without it. As she pulled it out to clean her nose, something small and square fell out and onto the side table that housed the flower arrangement.

Her head snapped in its direction, as did everybody else's.

Oh, no! One of the condoms she'd tucked into her purse had gotten tangled up with her handkerchief and fallen out. Instantly, Daniel's hand elegantly swooped in, captured the errant Trojan and put it in his jacket pocket as if he were picking up nothing more than a candy wrapper.

Sabrina caught his look. Oh God, she'd embarrassed him. His face seemed agitated. His cheeks turned red. Oh no, he was furious!

"I think it's getting late. Holly and I should head back. I've got a busy day ahead of me," Daniel abruptly said to Martin.

Yes, she'd embarrassed him, and now he wanted to leave. Both Martin and Nancy had clearly seen the condom but been polite enough not to comment on it. Sabrina was hoping for the ground in front of her to open up so she could disappear in it, but instead she felt Daniel's hand on the small of her back.

"Shall we, darling?" His voice was just as sweet as before. He was obviously trained in self control, keeping his anger in check while they were in the presence of their hosts.

She was in a daze when they said their goodbyes and Daniel led her out of the hall and back in the direction of the Mark Hopkins.

Sabrina felt horrible. She'd completely screwed up. This would get back to Misty, and then Holly would be in trouble. Instead of saving Holly's ass, she'd managed to get her even deeper into trouble. She had to try and salvage what she could, for Holly's sake.

"I'm so sorry," she started.

Daniel gave her a surprised look as he continued leading her across the foyer of the Mark Hopkins they'd just entered. "Sorry?"

"I really didn't mean to embarrass you. It was an accident." Her voice was pleading, and she hoped he could hear the sincerity in it. He'd have to accept her apology. She hadn't done it on purpose.

"Embarrass me?" He suddenly sounded bemused as he pressed the button for the elevator.

"Yes, I'm so sorry. I really didn't mean to. I should have been more careful," she rambled. She wasn't cut out to be an escort. Something was bound to go wrong, and it had.

The elevator was empty when they stepped inside. As soon as the door closed, Daniel turned back to her. "You didn't embarrass me. On the contrary."

Sabrina gave him a startled look. "But then why did we leave so suddenly?"

He let his gaze wander over her body. "Because I can think of something much better to do with the rest of the evening than hang out at a boring reception."

Daniel took a step toward her and placed his palm on the wall behind her. His head was only inches from hers, his eyes fixed on hers. She could smell his masculine scent, a faint mixture of cologne and man, and her stomach twisted itself into tiny knots.

"Oh." She couldn't say anything else, realization flooding her veins. The closeness of his body turned her brain into the consistency of porridge.

"You have to help me out here, Holly, but I haven't been with an escort before, so I'm not sure what the protocol is." She felt his breath on her face as he spoke to her in a low voice.

"Protocol?" she echoed breathlessly, being only too aware of his body virtually touching hers. She was pressed against the wall with nowhere to go.

"Yes. I don't know, but ... do you kiss?" His eyes were focused on her lips now. Had they been lasers, she would have been burned to a crisp within seconds.

"Y-yes," she stammered helplessly.

His hand came up to cup her jaw, lazily stroking her with his thumb. His touch was electrifying. Instinctively, her tongue snaked out to moisten her lips, and if he'd waited for a sign from her, this was it. Daniel lightly touched his lips to hers, and a faint sigh escaped her mouth. And then with one sweep, he captured her mouth fully, demanding her surrender.

His lips tugged on hers, suckling on her lower lip and pulling it into his mouth, where he swept over it with his moist tongue. He nibbled gently on her until she parted her lips, inviting his searching tongue inside her, expecting him.

Her hand went to the nape of his neck to pull him closer, when he couldn't get any closer than he already was. His body crushed hers against the wall of the elevator, barely leaving her space to breathe. But Sabrina didn't care. Who needed oxygen when she could inhale his scent instead?

Daniel tasted like a fresh shower in the middle of a rain forest, woodsy, vibrant, yet so dark, with layers of hidden treasures piled one on top of the other. And with every twirl of his tongue, he released yet another flavor, making her eager to capture his tongue with hers and imprison him within her.

***

Daniel couldn't believe what he was doing. He was kissing an escort, a prostitute. He'd probably lost his mind—and he knew exactly when it had happened. When she'd accidentally dropped the condom, he'd realized that what he'd paid for wasn't just to have a pretend girlfriend at the reception. She'd evidently been told by her agency to expect sex.

Who was he to disappoint her?

The way her mouth tasted made him feel intoxicated. He deepened his kiss, plundering her mouth and playing with her responsive tongue. Every time she moaned, the sound reverberated through his chest and filled him with eager anticipation of what was to come.

Holly had a way of turning him on as no other woman had ever managed to. He was a sexual guy, all right, but he generally needed more than two seconds of kissing to get fully aroused. She'd managed to arouse him with just that look she'd given him before he'd planted his lips onto hers.

She definitely knew what she was doing. After all, she was a professional. This was her job, to arouse men and please them. He could think of hundreds of ways how she could please him, but none of those ways were prudent in a hotel elevator.

As soon as the doors opened, Daniel pulled her out of the elevator with him. He looked at her face and saw that her cheeks were red, and her lips were plumper than before. He'd get back to those lips in a few seconds. But first, he had to get them into his room, away from prying eyes.

It seemed too long until they reached his room. Neither of them spoke, as if there was nothing to be said. Nothing that could be said in a public area anyway.

As soon as he let the door slam behind them, Daniel pulled her back into his arms and continued where he'd left off in the elevator. Those luscious lips needed more attention, and he was all too willing to give it to them. He put his thoughts about the fact that she was an escort aside. Right now, he didn't care. She was a woman, who excited him more than any woman had ever excited him, and he was only just kissing her.

He hadn't even touched her naked skin yet. He hadn't even kissed her breasts yet. And already he was as hard as an iron rod and yearning for release. If a woman could do that to him, he didn't care whether she was an escort or not. To hell with conventions.

Daniel took her wrists, fully encircling them with his hands and pulled them up to each side of her head, pressing them against the wall behind her. This woman brought out his most primal instincts. Her body pressed flush against the wall behind her, she looked vulnerable, yet her eyes were hungry, filled with desire.

Daniel ground his hips against her, making her aware of his need. Her response was a stifled moan as if she didn't want to admit she could feel him pressed against her through the thin fabric of her dress.

Instead, her head moved toward him, begging for another kiss. And he complied. How could he not? Holly was full of fire, and he had nothing to douse the fire with, only his own fuel to stoke the flames even more. Besides, he wasn't a fireman; he had no duty to put out a fire, and he sure wasn't going to put hers out, at least not until he had brought it to its roaring crescendo. And then some.

But he had to slow down before the entire room would combust and they'd start a fire which rivaled the one that had razed San Francisco in 1906.

Daniel tumbled to the couch with her and lowered himself, pulling her with him to rest on top of him as he stretched out, his lips never leaving hers. He could get drunk on her taste. Seriously drunk. Her kiss was pure sin. He pulled away for a second.

"Do you kiss every man like this? No. Don't answer that." No, he didn't want to think of the fact that this was what she did for a living, kiss strangers and have sex with them. No wonder she was so good. She had plenty of practice.

He sighed deeply.

"Is this ok?" Holly suddenly asked as he released her lips for a brief moment.

"Okay? I don't think I can ever go back to kissing an amateur after this."

"Amateur?"

"As opposed to a professional like you. Has nobody ever told you that your kisses can make a man commit every sin in the book?" He chuckled softly.

"And that's a good thing?" She sounded unsure, her green eyes searching his for an answer.

"Oh, yeah. That's a good thing."

Her lips curled into a smile, and he couldn't help but kiss it away and crush her lips with his mouth. His kiss became more demanding as he plundered her mouth greedily. His hand slid to the soft curves of her lower back, and he squeezed the swell of her ass, pressing her harder against his full-blown erection.

**

Through the thin fabric of her dress, Sabrina felt the outline of his body clearly, including his massive erection. She was amazed at how a man as gorgeous as he was could get turned on by her so quickly. She'd never considered herself a vixen. She knew she was pretty and had a decent figure, but she certainly wasn't a stunner like Holly.

But this man made her feel like she was the most desirable woman in the world. Wasn't it supposed to be the other way around? As an escort, wasn't *she* supposed to do the seducing? Instead, it felt like *he* was trying to seduce *her*. Maybe she should have gotten more detailed instructions from Holly. She could really screw this up.

And this was one thing she didn't want to screw up, not just for Holly's sake, but also for her own. Feeling Daniel's arms around her and his lips on her was the best thing that had happened to her in an eternity.

This man knew how to kiss and just how and where to touch a woman to make her melt under his hands. And there was no rush, no hasty movements despite the hunger she sensed in him. He allowed her to enjoy his touch and his kisses as if he got lost in them himself. No man had ever kissed her this thoroughly.

"Daniel," she murmured. His eyes dark with passion, he looked at her.

"Hmm?" he replied nibbling on her lower lip.

"Do you kiss every woman like this?" she teased him.

"You mean like this?" he asked and kissed her as if to brand her before releasing her a few minutes later.

"Uh-huh."

"What was the question?"

"Whether you kiss every—"

He interrupted her by capturing her mouth again, letting his tongue slide over her lips. "I can't answer any questions right now. I'm busy," he evaded her. "Or would you rather we talked instead?"

"No!"

***

Daniel laughed, and she blushed like a schoolgirl. He'd had no idea that escorts could find real pleasure in their work, but it was clear to him that she enjoyed what they were doing. She couldn't possibly be faking her body's responses to his touch. And then those quiet, barely-there moans she'd released. Almost inaudible, as if they were unintended. Had she wanted to fake her pleasure, she would have gone with a louder version. No, her reactions were real, and the knowledge fuelled his desire even more.

"What?" She gave him a confused look.

"You're beautiful."

There, she blushed again. Impossible to fake.

"I want to touch you."

She sat up, straddling him around his mid section. Slowly, her hands went behind her back to lower the zipper of her dress, but he stopped her.

"May I do that?"

She dropped her arms and nodded in approval. Daniel pulled himself up to sit, and his body touched hers. While his hands went to her back to work on the zipper, his lips weren't idle. Softly, they skimmed over her slender neck, tracing her skin with his tongue, gently nipping and grazing her skin with his teeth. She trembled under his touch.

Daniel worked his way along her shoulders and pushed the spaghetti strap of her dress over her arms. It fell easily now that he'd pulled down the zipper of her dress. Another pull and her dress pooled at her waist. He inched back to admire her naked breasts.

Perfect. Round and firm, no bra needed. Her dark pink nipples were hard. He needed to know what they felt like and allowed his hand to brush over them. She jerked as if she hadn't expected his touch. So sensitive. So responsive. A taste was what he needed.

Slowly, Daniel lowered his head until his mouth hovered over her nipple. His tongue swept over it in one smooth move before his lips encircled her hardened nipple and suckled slowly.

Her breathing instantly became heavier, faster, and he knew she was as aroused as he was. Her hands ran through his hair holding him to her body as if she didn't want him to stop. He wouldn't. He wanted everything she was willing to give him tonight. He would push her as far as she'd let him, and then he'd ask for more.

Daniel felt his erection strain against his pants and wasn't sure how long he'd be able to restrain himself, but he didn't want this to be over too quickly. For all he knew, all he'd get was only one act of sex with her. What if she left immediately after that? No, he had to make this last for a while.

Daniel wished he'd asked Tim more questions after he'd given him the details of the booking, but it was too late now. He'd just have to go along and hope he got what he wanted. And what he wanted was Holly, underneath him, on top of him, in front of him, every which way possible. Never before had he wanted a woman with such intensity.

Daniel kneaded her neglected breast while he continued sucking and gently biting the other one before he switched and inflicted the same sweet torture on the other. She didn't suppress her moans, and he relished her body's response to him.

"Oh, Daniel, that's so ..." She didn't finish her sentence, either because she ran out of breath or because her brain had turned to the same mush as his. He couldn't think of anything else but to kiss her, touch her, be with her. All rational thoughts had gone out the window the moment she'd dropped the condom.

"Holly, tell me what you want."

Her eyes flew open. "What I want?"

What had made him ask that? She was the escort. He shouldn't be asking her what she wanted. It wasn't his job to pleasure her, but the other way around. Yet, he wanted to please her. "Yes, I want to know what you like."

***

"You're doing a pretty good job turning me into putty without any instructions." As soon as she'd said it, Sabrina wanted to take it back. How could she have said something that exposed her like this, something that made her so vulnerable?

"Yes, but imagine what I could do if you told me what you really liked." He gave her a wicked grin.

Daniel Sinclair was definitely something else. What man hired an escort and then insisted on pleasuring her rather than letting her do the job? What the hell was wrong with him? Or had Holly completely misrepresented what her job was like? It wasn't like her to lie about these things. No, something was wrong with this man.

Before he could sink his lips back onto her breasts, she cupped his face and pulled him up.

"Why?"

"Why what?"

"Why do you want to know what I like?"

"Because I think this night is going to be much more fun if we're both satisfied. Don't you think so?" Their gazes locked. "And besides, what man wouldn't like to be considered the best lover a woman has ever had? So maybe you want to help me out here a little?"

Sabrina laughed. She had the feeling he didn't really need any help to be the best lover she ever had. He was doing a damn fine job so far. But she wasn't about to tell him that. If he wanted to try harder, she'd let him.

"Is that a yes?"

She nodded. "Do you think we could move to …?" She made a head movement toward the bedroom.

"Your wish is my command."

***

Seconds later, Daniel lifted her up and carried her to the bedroom. Now the real fun would start, the slow undressing, the teasing, the seduction. Not that he hadn't enjoyed kissing Holly, he had, more than any other woman he'd ever met. But now she lay on his bed, and there was no turning back from it.

Her bare breasts exposed to his hungry eyes, her nipples hardened, she looked up at him through her long dark lashes that guarded those tempting green eyes. She made him feel like the wolf, who wanted to devour the lamb, the very willing lamb.

Slowly, Daniel took off his jacket and threw it onto a nearby chair. He didn't care that it would be creased tomorrow. It didn't matter. Button after button of his shirt he eased open as she watched him silently as if fascinated by the simple action of a man undressing. When he dropped the shirt to the floor, he caught her tongue licking her lips.

He kicked off his shoes and dropped down onto the bed covering her body with his.

"Miss me?"

"I missed your lips," she confessed.

He didn't know why he said ridiculous things to her, but he liked the way she responded. There was a truth and a simplicity in her answers that floored him. Things seemed to be simple with her, black and white, uncomplicated. Nothing high maintenance about her. No frills, just pure woman.

It appealed to his masculinity, to his darker, animalistic side, his true passions. It awakened the side of him that for the most part was dormant. The side that lived for the hunt to satisfy his carnal desires. His need to possess a woman, one hundred percent. And for her to possess him, something he had never let a woman do, because he'd always held back, never given all of himself. Never dared.

This time, all he wanted was to take this woman and possess her completely and give himself to her completely without holding back. This was the first time he'd be safe, safe from any emotions that could result, safe from any future implications. Because she'd be gone the next day, and he'd never see her again. That's why he could give her everything inside of him.

"Forget who and what you are. Tonight you're just a woman, and I'm a man. That's all that's important."

There was a glimpse of something in her eyes that looked like agreement or recognition, he wasn't sure. When she sought his lips, he knew she was ready for anything. Her hands touched his smooth back and stroked his hot skin. Wherever she touched him, Daniel felt as if a trail of molten lava was left behind.

He rolled them to the side to relieve her of his weight and to let his hands glide around her body. Pushing the fabric of her dress further down her back, he slipped his hands underneath it to find the gentle curves of her perfectly formed ass. The panties she wore were of simple cotton, no lace, no frills. Yet so inviting.

A gentle moan escaped her lips as he pulled her panties down a few inches to rest them at the apex of her thighs, just enough to expose the twin swells that reminded him of Twin Peaks overlooking San Francisco. He ran his hand over them to feel the softness of her skin, just like velvet.

He'd go slowly and take his time to explore every inch of her divine body before he'd consume her. Daniel separated his lips from hers and felt her reluctance to do so, but as soon as his lips went lower to attend to her breasts instead, she let out another sigh. With his teeth, he tugged at her nipple, feeling her quiver beneath him before he smoothed the tender spot with his tongue.

He knew how to gently torture a woman, how to elicit wanton reactions from her, how to make her gasp with pleasure. Daniel sucked her breast like a babe that would never be weaned off, and still Holly arched her back to ask for more, thrusting more of her breast into his mouth, demanding that he suck harder.

"Oh, please, yes!"

She literally begged him for more, digging her fingers into his shoulders to hold him close to her. He'd asked her what she liked, and it seemed she'd found her voice to tell him. Daniel wasn't one to ignore her wishes, and bestowed the same attention on her other breast, leaving her nipples tender to the touch.

He ignored his aching erection begging to be let out of the confinement of his pants. He knew if he gave in, it would be over too soon. There was too much he wanted to do with her, so he suppressed his need for now. It would be even sweeter to take her once he'd waited long enough.

What he couldn't ignore any longer though, was the aroma of her arousal. Dropping his lips down to her stomach, he soaked in the tempting scent, inhaling deeply. There was something primal about her scent, something unspoiled and pure. Pure woman, no games.

His hands grabbed hold of her dress and pulled it down over her hips, exposing her body fully to him except for the small area between her legs still coved with the tiny speck of fabric. With his teeth, he pulled at the fabric and nudged it down to expose her dark curls underneath. Then he used his hands to rid her of her panties completely.

Willingly, she let him proceed.

"Oh, God, Holly, you're beautiful." He glanced up at her. Her eyes were half closed, her lips parted. "I have to taste you." It wasn't a question or a demand, not even a request. It was just a statement of an inevitable action he had to perform as if compelled by a higher power. As soon as he sank his face into her female center and soaked in her enticing aroma, he knew he was lost.

His tongue lapped against her warm and glistening flesh, licking at the moisture oozing from her. Eagerly, she spread her legs for him to allow him closer access, gasping when he repeated his tender strokes. His fingers spread her before him as he greedily continued his quest to explore every nook and cranny with his tongue.

Holly twisted and flexed under his mouth, and he scooped his hands under her sweet ass to press her more firmly into him. No, she wouldn't escape him. For tonight, she was his.

"Mine, all mine," he whispered into her flesh, before he plunged his tongue into her inviting pussy. He bathed in the heat emanating from her center, drank from her moisture and inhaled her scent. She was becoming part of his body, and he knew he'd recognize her scent a hundred years from now if he were to live that long.

Withdrawing his tongue from her center, he knew there was another place he wanted to taste. He'd left the best for last. His tongue moved upwards to the small but fully engorged nub of flesh hidden at the base of her curls. In slow motion, he grazed the spot with his tongue and instantly felt her tremble.

She was more sensitive than a seismograph. Daniel's lips formed into a smile. When he was done with her she'd have been though a 9.5 magnitude earthquake, he could almost guarantee it. And he'd also guarantee massive aftershocks rippling through her. And his own body would be caught up in each and every one of those earthquakes she'd be experiencing. The famous 1906 San Francisco earthquake would register as a gentle ripple on a pond compared to what she'd be feeling.

"Baby, you'd better hold on tight." It was only fair to give her advance warning.

***

What was he trying to do to her? Sabrina had never felt anything like it. This man, who was practically a stranger, was inflicting the most delicious torture she'd ever experienced. She'd had no idea that sex could be this good, and he was still half dressed and hadn't even penetrated her yet.

The fact that she was completely naked in the arms of a gorgeous stranger, who seemed to have put it into his head to give her every conceivable pleasure in his power, seemed surreal. But it was real, as real as his hot breath caressing her clit before his tongue stroked over it again and again in a rhythm as old as time.

She knew what he was doing, and had he been any other man, she would have pulled back and withdrawn at the intimacy of his action, but because he was a stranger and she was pretending to be somebody else, she let herself go and surrendered to his tempting caress. She allowed herself to feel and not think.

Daniel's tongue was relentless, but when he explored her with his fingers and slowly drove one into her, she almost leapt off the bed at the intense sensation. She hadn't felt a man inside her in such a long time. And if his finger could create such an emotion in her, she could only guess what would happen when she'd finally feel his cock inside her. Sabrina shivered instinctively.

He slid his finger smoothly in and out of her slick flesh. With every movement, more moisture pooled in her center, more heat built up within her. She felt like a volcano ready to explode, ready to blow its top.

And she felt completely and utterly vulnerable and didn't care that she was. He wouldn't hurt her. After tonight, she'd never see him again. There would be no embarrassment, no possibility of being hurt by him. He would never even know her name.

"Come for me, baby," she heard him whisper.

Daniel's fingers worked her frantically. His tongue played with her clit, and he knew just the right rhythm to drive her to the edge. She felt her excitement build, her breathing become more ragged. It was time to let go of her control and hand it over to him, surrender to him and do what he demanded.

When his tongue lapped against her clit again and his finger hit her g-spot at the same time, she was past the point of no return. Like a tsunami building out in the ocean, she felt a faint tingle start in her belly and ripple outward until it crashed against the wave that had started in her extremities, powering together in a massive crescendo, exploding in the center of her body. Flowing outward wave after wave, the ripples wouldn't stop.

There was no end to it, nor to the scream she heard in her ears, a scream of release coming from her own throat. Whether her orgasm lasted seconds or minutes, she was unaware of time and place. She only knew she'd never felt anything like it. She'd never felt this free.

As if in a fog, she felt Daniel move up her body and cradle her against his chest until her body finally returned to normal. When Sabrina opened her eyes again, she looked into the smiling face of her lover.

"Oh. My. God."

"I'm glad you liked the appetizer. How about we move on to the main course?" He beamed unashamedly.

She shook her head slowly. "Not before you've tasted *your* appetizer."

Sabrina tugged at the button of his pants. "I want you naked, now."

Whether Daniel minded being commanded by a woman or not, she didn't know. But for what it was worth, she'd never seen a man get rid of his pants and boxers that quickly.

Before he had a chance to lower himself back onto the bed, though, she stopped him. He stood right in front of the bed, his erection proudly jutting out in front of him. His body was perfect. His broad chest was hairless down to his navel, where a small trail of dark hair started and led to the nest of curls surrounding his shaft.

His stomach was flat, and while he didn't quite have a six-pack, he was lean and muscular as if he took good care of his body. She would make sure to take good care of his body tonight.

"Beautiful." Sabrina admired him and reached out her hand to touch him. Despite his hardness, his skin was soft, and the head of his enormous shaft felt like velvet. He moaned at the first touch of her fingers on him. As she kneeled before him on the bed, her head was at the perfect height for what she wanted to do.

Quickly glancing at his face, she made sure he knew what he was in for. The hungry look in his eyes told her that not only did he know what she was planning, but he could barely wait.

Like a Greek God, he stood before her. And she would make him surrender to her with as little as her tongue and her mouth. Slowly and seductively, she moved toward him until his erection was less than half an inch from her lips. Her tongue made the first contact, lapping tenderly at the very tip of his shaft, then sliding down his length.

Daniel gasped loudly, making her smile. Yes, she could reduce him to putty just like he'd done with her. And nothing could stop her from doing just that. But she'd make him beg for it. She wanted nothing more right now than to hear him begging for her mouth to bury him.

"More?" Sabrina asked him.

"Oh, God, yes." His voice was hoarse and had nothing in common with the voice with which he'd made conversation at the reception.

"More?" He hadn't begged yet.

"Oh, please, Holly, put me out of my misery!"

Instantly, she licked him from tip to base and back, then took him into her mouth and moved down his cock, taking him as deep as she could. She felt him shudder. His taste was a hint salty, mixed with a very primal essence that was all him, something she couldn't describe. Sabrina had given blowjobs before, but never really enjoyed it. This was different.

Knowing that she could bring him to his knees with a stroke of her tongue or the gentle sucking of her lips closing around his erection, made her feel powerful and incredibly turned on. Soon the pulsating cock in her mouth would fill her core and rock her very center of gravity, and her muscles would clench around him to milk him until he had nothing more to give. But for now, she'd only drive him to the point where he couldn't think straight anymore.

***

Daniel's hands went to her shoulders, holding on to balance himself as he rocked back and forth in synch with her rhythm. His eyes closed, his head thrown back, he let himself go. She made it easy for him to only feel what his body wanted him to feel and forget his mind, forget his work, his goals, and only remember that he was a man in the hands of a beautiful woman.

Her mouth around his hard cock was warm and moist. Her tongue played with his skin, tickling and teasing him. This was not the kind of mechanical blowjob he'd received from his ex-girlfriends, no, this was something entirely different. This was the mouth of a woman, who was in it with every fiber of her body.

Holly wasn't just going through the motions. The way she sucked him, licked him and teasingly grazed him with her teeth without hurting him, he knew she wanted to give him the best blowjob he'd ever had. And she was succeeding. She pulled harder, sucking him deeper into her mouth, and he realized that he couldn't go much longer. This was too good.

Daniel didn't want to come in her mouth, at least not the first time. He needed to be inside her and feel her muscles tighten around him when he came. And he needed to look into her eyes when he did so. He needed to lose himself in those beautiful green eyes.

The way she sucked his cock drove him insane, and he felt his control slipping. Before it was too late, he pulled himself out of her mouth and held her back, away from him.

"I wasn't done," she complained and pouted. Cute.

"Baby, you're killing me." He brought her up him and kissed her plump lips. "Let me be inside of you."

She pulled him down onto the bed with her. He stopped in mid-motion.

"Wait."

She gave him a questioning look.

"Condom." He snatched his jacket off the chair and pulled the condom out of its pocket before joining her on the bed.

"May I?" she asked and pointed at the condom.

He shook his head. As if he could survive her touch. "I won't last if I let you touch me right now."

He was walking a tightrope. Any second, he could lose his control and give into the release that he felt so close to the surface. He had to have her, and he couldn't wait another second. Daniel sheathed himself with the condom and pulled her back into his arms.

Her body molded to his perfectly as if she were made for him. His erection nudged at the entrance to her body, and he locked eyes with hers. As he slowly slid into her inch by inch, he lost himself in the depth of her eyes. He had to watch her as he entered her. He had to see her reaction, see what she felt.

What he saw in her eyes was pleasure, desire, and passion. Nobody could fake that. He captured her lips with his, and thrust into her to the hilt, slicing through her body as through butter. Holly was tighter that he'd expected. How she kept her muscles so tight around his cock surprised him. She felt as tight as a virgin, not the professional escort she was.

Daniel stayed buried in her for several long seconds, unable to move for fear he'd lose it right there and then. Finally, he felt his strength return and was able to move inside her. Slick flesh on slick flesh, their bodies moved in synch with each other. Pulling out almost entirely, he slammed into her again a second later as she met his thrust with an equal but opposite reaction, only intensifying his movement.

Being inside her was a slide into slickness and warmth but with the tightness of a glove one size too small, accommodating his size with an extraordinarily snug fit. As if she'd been built for him and for him alone. Every time he pulled out so only the very tip of his cock was still submerged in her heat, she begged for him to fill her again, and every time he did so, and did so completely.

Daniel knew he'd met his match when she used his weight against him, hooking her leg behind him and rolling him over. As she sat up, keeping his erection deeply buried inside her, she gave him a wanton smile.

The sight of her naked body straddling him, her boobs bouncing with every move she made, was beyond his strained control. Every time she moved upwards and then down again, his hips moved up to meet her, pounding into her with as much force as his position allowed. It wasn't enough. He was near his breaking point and needed more.

"Oh, baby."

Daniel rolled them and flipped her onto her back again. "Please, come with me."

His hand went between their bodies finding the little nub of pleasure he was so familiar with by now and caressed her as he plunged into her over and over, matching the rhythm of their beating hearts and their labored breaths until he finally felt her muscles clench around his cock. It was perfect. Her spasms ignited his own release, and he exploded like an erupting volcano.

As their climaxes ebbed, their bodies stilled. Breathing hard, he gazed at her.

"You're amazing," he was able to mumble despite the little energy he had left.

"Likewise," she rasped.

And then he kissed her, lazily, tenderly, without an end in sight. His tongue explored her mouth as if it had never invaded before, dancing with her the timid dance of two high school kids, and entangled itself with its counterpart as if to create another Gordian knot.

There was no demand in his kiss, no intent for it to lead to anything else. It was a means and an end in itself. A kiss. A kiss full of tenderness and appreciation, of adoration and respect. A timeless caress.

Only reluctantly, he released her from their kiss.

"Oh, my God, what was this?" she whispered breathlessly, her eyes gazing into his.

Daniel smiled. "Dessert."

Chapter Four

It was past midnight, and Holly had gotten dressed. While she was in the bathroom, Daniel retrieved his wallet and took out several hundred dollar bills. He'd already paid the agency, but he didn't feel it was enough. What she'd given him tonight was beyond what he'd expected. Never had he been able to lose himself as he had with her, and never had he felt a woman give herself so completely to him.

Daniel looked back at the tangled sheets on the bed, witnesses to their passionate encounter. She'd awakened in him what it meant to be alive. His life had been consumed with work, and he'd forgotten how to enjoy himself, how to relax and how to love. She'd shown him there was more to life than work.

He placed the money into an envelope together with a simple note, sealed it and slipped it into her purse, not wanting to taint their goodbyes with the exchange of money.

She came out of the bathroom and was ready to leave. Their lovemaking was written all over her body. She seemed to glow. Silently, he put his arm around her waist and led her to the door, then turned her toward him and pulled her close to his body.

Without a word, he sought her lips and found her eagerly accepting his kiss. One last time, his tongue swept through her mouth, visiting the places he knew so intimately by now. He felt her hands in his hair, and he loved the feel of it. It felt too good to stop.

Reluctantly, he pulled away from her and looked into her green eyes which seemed so much darker after their night of passion.

"You'd better leave before I drag you back into bed and have my way with you." His voice was hoarse and dark with desire. He was a fool for letting her leave, and he knew it.

"I thought I had my way with you," she teased him.

"Same difference."

Once the door closed behind her, Daniel let himself fall against it and exhaled deeply. She was gone but had left him with the realization that he wasn't as cold and indifferent as some of his ex-girlfriends had accused him of being. He could clearly feel the fire in is belly, the fire she'd ignited.

***

Sabrina staggered toward the elevator, her legs still shaking from the intense encounter. She'd tried to compose herself in his bathroom—to no avail. She was a mess, and the signs of sex were clearly written all over her body: her ruffled hair, her flushed face, the love bites he'd left on her skin, the pleasant humming between her legs, the scent of Daniel on her skin.

She was certain that anybody she'd run into on her way home would instantly know that she'd just had the most mind-blowing sex of her life. She was relieved to see that the elevator was empty but dreaded the moment she had to cross the lobby, where the hotel staff could surely guess that she'd been in a guest's room to have sex.

Pearls of sweat built on her forehead. Sabrina opened her purse to pull out her handkerchief to pat herself dry and instantly noticed an unfamiliar item in it. She pulled out the envelope she knew hadn't been there earlier.

Curiously she opened it. In it were several hundred dollar bills and a handwritten note.

Thank you for the most wonderful night. Daniel.

Sabrina knew she couldn't accept the money. She couldn't accept money for something that had made her feel like a real woman again. No man had ever given her so much pleasure in her life, and she wasn't going to let him sully this feeling by taking his money. Yes, he'd paid the agency, but she would tell Holly to keep that. She didn't want a penny of it.

What she'd given Daniel tonight, she'd given freely, and what she had received in turn from him, was more than she'd expected to ever receive from any man, let alone from one, who thought she was an escort.

His tenderness, his passion, his selflessness in pleasing her were things she'd never seen in any of the men she'd dated. Why a man who believed her to be an escort would treat her with such care, she couldn't even begin to comprehend.

In the foyer, she wrote a note to Daniel, slipped it into a new envelope she picked up from the front desk and placed the money in it before she sealed it. She was careful so the front desk staff didn't see what she'd put in the envelope.

"Could you please give this to Mr. Sinclair in 2307 in the morning?"

"Certainly, madam," the employee answered and took the envelope from her. He looked her up and down, and she wondered what he was thinking. Was she a sugar mama, who was paying off her gigolo? Not even close.

Sabrina quickly left the lobby and stepped into a waiting cab.

Holly was waiting for her when she came home. As soon as Sabrina unlocked the front door, she heard her friend call out to her from the living room.

"Sabrina, is everything ok?"

She walked toward the living room and stopped at the door. Holly was propped up on the couch, a dry biscuit in one hand and a cup of tea on the coffee table.

"Are you feeling better?"

Holly waved her off. "Much better. Now, tell me, what happened? I didn't expect you to be out so long."

Sabrina smiled coyly. "He was very nice."

"What? Very nice? You think you can dish me off with *very nice*? I want the whole story."

Holly patted the space next to her on the couch, signaling to Sabrina to sit down.

"I'm really tired. I should go to bed." Her resistance was met with a stern look by Holly.

"Oh, no, you won't. Not until you've given me the dirt."

Sabrina felt her cheeks turn hot. Her friend could be a pest when she wanted to know something.

"You had sex with him," Holly stated the obvious. "No, wait! You had fabulous sex with him!"

Sabrina couldn't suppress her smile.

"Oh my God! Sit down, and tell me everything."

She only told Holly what was absolutely necessary and didn't go into any of the intimate details of her night with Daniel. She wanted those things to be her own, because she knew that this was all she would get, one fabulous night with an amazing man. She didn't want to share this experience, not even with her best friend.

She was certain Holly realized that she was holding things back from her, but after a half hour she didn't press her any longer.

***

Daniel woke from the best sleep he'd had in years. The sun shone into his bedroom since he'd neglected to close the drapes the night before. Instead of jumping out of bed instantly the moment he woke as he normally did, he folded his hands behind his head and stared at the ceiling. Then he gazed around the room.

His clothes were strewn all over the floor. Holly's scent was still all around him, on his skin, on his lips, in the sheets. The memories of the night would see him through the next few weeks until he finalized the deal and then refocused his life. He'd done a lot of thinking since she'd left.

She'd reminded him that he was a passionate man and that he needed a passionate woman. He'd inherited more than his olive skin from his mother. He'd inherited her passion as well. He remembered the heated arguments she and his father had from time to time. As a teenager, Daniel had always cringed when he saw them afterwards as they ran off to their bedroom and locked the door behind them. Their lovemaking had been just as passionate as their fights, and Daniel had moved his room to the other side of the house once the *ick* factor had become too much for him.

Only now, he understood what they were going through. He had felt the same passion in himself.

When he was back in New York he'd do something about it, try to find a woman to complete his life. Maybe he could fulfill one of his mother's wishes after all: *bambini.* But for now, he needed to concentrate on the deal.

After a long shower, Daniel got dressed and made his way down into the lobby to get to his first meeting of the day. Before he could ask the doorman to call him a taxi, a hotel employee tapped him on the shoulder.

"Mr. Sinclair. This was left for you last night." The man handed him an envelope. His name was handwritten on it. The letter felt rather thick to the touch.

"Thank you." Curiously, he opened it, discovering cash together with a note. He read it and stopped in his tracks.

Daniel. You've given me too much already.

It wasn't signed. Holly. She'd rejected his gift. He didn't understand why, and he had no time to think about it now. He had to get to his meeting.

The entire morning, he didn't have a single minute to reflect on Holly's note. Several new issues were raised regarding a contingency that hadn't yet been met, and he needed to concentrate on the issue at hand. Everything could still fall apart if he wasn't careful now. Too many things were riding on this deal.

Daniel was glad when it was time for lunch. He'd arranged to meet Tim at a downtown restaurant. They'd met the night he'd flown in and already caught up on the latest events, particularly on the breakup with Audrey.

"You look exhausted, Danny." Tim was the only one who called him Danny besides his parents. With his blonde shaggy hair, Tim was the picture of a surfer dude and didn't look a bit like the financial whiz kid he actually was.

"Didn't get much sleep." A wicked grin stole itself onto his lips.

Tim immediately caught on. "You dog! You fucked the escort. Who would have thought?"

He simply shrugged. "Don't make a big deal out of it. She was cute." She was more than cute, but he wasn't about to share his experience, not even with his best friend.

"So, tell me more."

"Get your kicks out of somebody else, Tim. I'm not sharing my sex life."

"You have a sex life with an escort?"

"Subject closed." He changed tracks. "Thanks for setting me up with the attorneys. I'll meet them tomorrow morning. Just as well, we're running into a few snags with some of the contingencies."

"Anything major?" Tim had a business mind just as sharp as Daniel's and was always at hand to bounce ideas off of.

"Nothing the attorneys won't be able to manage. But I'll probably have to stay a little longer than I anticipated."

"Sounds good to me. Hey, a few buddies and I are going to see a show tonight. I'm sure we can get you an extra ticket. The cast is from London and—"

"Sorry, can't. I've got plans already." He didn't, but he was about to make plans. The note Holly had left intrigued him. She was an escort. She worked for money, so why hadn't she taken his tip? What escort in her right mind would reject extra money?

***

Holly was anxiously awaiting Sabrina when she returned home.

"About time!"

Sabrina gave her a stunned look. It was only about six o'clock, her usual time to return from work. "What's wrong?" She was instantly on alert.

"He requested you again."

Her heart missed a beat. She didn't need to ask who *he* was.

"For tonight. You have to get ready now." Holly was all excited and literally jumped in the air.

"But, I can't. This was a one night thing. I can't continue doing this." As much as she'd enjoyed the night with him, she couldn't continue pretending to be Holly.

"Sweetie, you've got to. If I show up instead of you, he'll call the agency, and Misty will find out. She'll fire me. Please. I'm sure this is the last time. He's from New York. He'll go back in a few days." Holly's voice was pleading. "Have I ever asked you for anything?"

She was right. She'd never asked for any favors apart from the one last night and now this one. Actually, it was really just one favor stretched over two nights.

Sabrina felt torn. One side of her wanted to see Daniel again and continue where they'd left off, the other was scared of the consequences. She couldn't get involved with him, not with a man who slept with escorts, well, okay, pretend escorts.

"Holly, please. This won't work."

"You liked him. You said the sex was good. So, please just do this for me. Just tonight."

Against her better judgment, she felt herself nod. "But this is the last time."

"Promise."

***

An hour later, Sabrina met Daniel in the hotel lobby. He was dressed in black jeans and a casual shirt and looked even more handsome than he had the night before. He looked up from his newspaper when she entered the lobby and jumped up instantly.

With a few strides, he was there to greet her. He took her hand into his.

"Hi."

"Hi," she echoed back.

"I hope you're hungry. We're having dinner at a place near Telegraph Hill."

Sabrina gave him a surprised look. "We're going out? Am I playing your fiancée again?"

Daniel shook his head. "We're going out just the two of us." He let his eyes glide over her body before resting them on her lips again. "And we're coming back here later."

The searing look in his eyes was a promise she'd hold him to.

A taxi took them to their destination, and during the entire cab ride Daniel held her hand. When he helped her out of the taxi, his body brushed against hers, and she shivered slightly. Her nipples instantly hardened.

"Miss me?" he whispered into her ear but didn't wait for a reply. "Come."

Daniel led her inside. It wasn't what she'd expected. It wasn't a restaurant but a large kitchen. Several other couples were assembled as well as three chefs dressed in customary chef's garb.

"Welcome to Tante Marie's Cooking School."

Sabrina shot him an astounded look and caught him grin. "I've always wanted to try this," he whispered to her. "It'll be fun."

***

Tim had told him about the place and that they offered dinner cooking classes for couples. It was so far removed from what Daniel normally did on a date that he thought it would be perfect. He wanted to do something different, and he wanted to get to know Holly and understand why she'd rejected his money. He figured the relaxed atmosphere at a cooking class was the perfect place to do just that.

The menu was simple: a salad, handmade pizza, and a tiramisu. Plenty of wine both during the cooking and during dinner. Enough to loosen anybody's tongue.

The chefs first demonstrated the preparation of the dishes then assigned the duties to the different couples before they were let loose on the tasks. He and Holly had the task of making pizza dough. Following the recipe to a *t*, they measured the ingredients, mixed them with a spoon in a large bowl, and then emptied them out onto a large wooden board.

"Do you want to knead or shall I?" she asked him.

"Why don't you start on it, and when your hands get tired I'll take over." Daniel stood right next to her watching her every move. They both had donned aprons the school had provided.

Her elegant hands worked through the dough, and he watched her, fascinated. Silently, he stepped behind her and molded his body to hers. He felt her surprise, but she didn't move away.

She fit perfectly into his chest, and he knew instinctively that he would have the best sleep of his life if he could only spoon her and nuzzle his head in the crook of her neck. That's what he wanted, have her stay with him the entire night and fall asleep with her cradled in his arms. Later, when they were back at his hotel, he'd ask her to stay until morning.

Reaching his hands forward, he put them onto hers and helped her knead the dough while he put his cheek to hers.

"Why didn't you take my money last night?"

She stiffened.

"You deserved it," he assured her and continued moving her hands with his through the dough.

"You didn't need to give me anything."

"Why?"

"It was more than enough."

"What was more than enough?"

"What you gave me last night."

Daniel needed to get to the bottom of this. "The money I paid to the agency?"

"No. That's not what I meant."

"Please, Holly. What did you mean?"

"Nobody has ever made me feel this good."

His hands stopped. "But—"

"Nobody," she repeated and turned her head to look at him. "You're the best lover I've ever had."

Looking into her green eyes, he believed her. His mouth found hers without thinking. He lost himself in a deep kiss. Hungry as he was, he all but devoured her, losing any sense of time and place.

**

Sabrina wasn't sure whether she should have told him, but he'd been so insistent, and at this point what would be the harm if she told him the truth? And the truth was he was the best lover she'd ever had. Not that she'd had that many, but even if she had, she was sure that he would still be the best.

When she felt his demanding lips on hers, she wished they were back at his hotel, where she could rip his clothes off. She felt more than aroused by his kiss and felt her panties getting soaked with warm moisture oozing from her core.

"Hey, lovebirds, are we going to get that pizza dough any time soon?" a voice pulled them out of their embrace. The couple who was assigned with preparing the toppings for the pizza grinned at them.

Daniel chuckled. "Pizza dough, coming right up." And then he gave her another searing look and whispered just for her to hear, "We'll continue this later."

Sabrina so desperately wanted to sit down to stop her knees from shaking. How this man could turn her weak like this with just one kiss was beyond her. Daniel gave her a knowing look. Oh yes, he knew exactly the kind of effect he had on her. Maybe it had been a bad idea after all to tell him that he was her best lover. Like he needed any more encouragement.

The food was better than they would have eaten at a five star restaurant. They sat together at a long communal table with the other couples, chatting, drinking and complimenting each other on their cooking skills.

They were engaged in a conversation with the couple sitting opposite them, who had introduced themselves as Kim and Marcus.

"You guys are either newlyweds or engaged to be married, am I right?" Kim asked curiously. Her husband nudged her in the ribs.

"Don't be so nosy, honey."

"That's quite all right," Daniel replied. "So, what makes you think that, Kim?"

"You guys obviously can't keep your hands off each other, no offense. That's what we were like at the beginning too. Do you remember, honey?" Kim gave her husband a sheepish look.

"Sure do," he replied and planted a wet kiss on her neck. She laughed out loud.

"Sorry, Marcus is obviously regressing to that time."

He grunted humorously. "Where did you guys meet?"

"A friend's party."

"Internet," Daniel said almost simultaneously.

Sabrina shot Daniel a nervous look.

"I mean, I was going to sign up for some internet dating service," Daniel back-peddled.

"But then, my friend threw a party for all her single friends," Sabrina helped him.

"And we were supposed to all write up our bios at that party. You know, how we were going to describe ourselves for that internet dating service. And Holly helped me write up my bio, and one thing led to the next."

Good save. She smiled at him, and he smiled back.

"That's hilarious," Kim exclaimed. "I'm curious. How did you describe him?"

Sabrina had more improvising to do. But this was easier than she thought. She would just describe him the way she saw him right now.

"Handsome Adonis seeks Goddess of Love on whom to bestow carnal pleasures in exchange for undying love and devotion." The words rolled easily off her lips, surprising herself.

She caught Daniel's stunned look.

"Wow!" Kim's voice came from across the table.

"And that's when I realized that my Goddess of Love was sitting right next to me, so we left the party without signing up for the internet dating service," Daniel added and gave her another hungry look.

After dessert was served, it quieted down, and they left the school, escaping into the fresh evening air.

"Thank you," Sabrina said to him. "It was so much fun. Come, now I want to show you something."

He raised an eyebrow. "What do you want to show me?"

"A fabulous view over the Bay, and it's only a block away from here." She knew of a staircase, hidden away off Green Street, which ran in between several homes and ended at a little viewing platform affording a breathtaking view over the Bay. They walked up the steep street and came to a halt midway.

The staircase was to their left, but to Sabrina's surprise there was an iron gate blocking the entry.

"Oh, no, it's locked." She was disappointed. It would have been romantic to look out over the city and the Bay from up there. She turned away. "That's a shame."

***

Daniel saw her disappointed look and pulled her back. There would be no disappointments tonight. "How do you feel about trespassing?"

"Trespassing? You wouldn't!"

"Why not?" He felt like a rascal as he grinned sheepishly.

"We could get arrested!"

"As long as they lock us up in the same cell, I don't care. Come, take off your shoes, and I'll lift you over the gate."

Daniel wouldn't take no for an answer. He bent down and slipped one shoe off her foot, then made her lift the other leg to free her from her other shoe. Since he was already down at her feet he thought nothing of using the opportunity to run his tongue from her ankle to her knee.

She panted heavily, and he gave her a suggestive look. He loved making her all nervous and shaky. "So, do you want me to help you over the gate, or do you want me to kiss every inch of your body right here in full view of every passerby?" He gave her a look that would tell her that he had every intention of carrying out his threat.

"Over the gate," she exclaimed quickly.

Within seconds, he'd helped her over the four-foot high gate and handed the shoes back to her before lifting himself over it.

The fifty-or-so steps led to a small platform surrounded by wooden balustrades on three sides and a retaining wall at the back. There was also a park bench to sit.

Daniel certainly enjoyed the view toward Alcatraz, the Bay Bridge and the lights across the Bay, but what he enjoyed even more was Holly's body standing in front of him, braced against the railing. His hands snaked around her waist and pulled her into him.

Her contours fit perfectly to his chest. "How many other people do you think might trespass here tonight?"

"I don't think anybody is as crazy as you."

"Good. That means we have privacy up here." He knew she was aware what he needed privacy for, because a second later his hand went to her breast and captured it. With his mouth, he took hold of the strap of her dress and pulled it over her shoulder. The fabric that had covered her breast dropped, and his hand stroked her naked skin.

While he teased her nipple with his fingers and turned it hard, his other hand reached under her skirt.

"Why don't you lose those panties?" His voice was hoarse, and he pressed his growing erection against her. Daniel knew what they were doing was crazy, but she didn't stop him. Being out in the open with her, touching her the way he did made him hornier than a sixteen year old high school kid having discovered Playboy magazine.

As soon as Holly stepped out of her panties, he grabbed them and put them into his jeans pocket. "You'll get those back at the hotel." Maybe. But most likely not. Like an Indian warrior kept a scalp, he'd keep her panties.

"We shouldn't be doing this here." Her protest was weak at best, and he ignored it.

He still stood behind her. "No screaming this time, as much as I love to hear it," he cautioned her. God, how he'd enjoyed the scream she'd released when he'd first brought her to climax the night before. Raw and untamed. Full of life, full of passion.

Daniel dropped down to his knees behind her and lifted her dress to admire the cutest ass he'd ever had the pleasure to touch. His hands stroked gently over her soft skin. Within seconds, he felt goose bumps and a soft sigh escaping her lips.

He brushed his lips against her skin and licked his tongue over her cheeks, squeezing them gently with his hands.

"Oh, Daniel."

"Yes, baby?"

"You're insane."

One hand went between her thighs heading for her warm core. His fingers slid along the familiar folds of her moist flesh before they found her inviting entrance. Too impatient to wait, he plunged one finger into her.

"Not doing *this* would be insane," Daniel corrected her.

She gasped at the force of his penetration. He continued to lavish her ass with kisses all the while continuing to move his finger back and forth, in and out of her slick flesh. Then he added a second finger, intensifying the sensation and continued sliding in and out of her.

His erection strained against his pants, the zipper painfully biting into his hard length. She'd gotten him hornier tonight than he'd been in a long time, and he couldn't wait to be inside of her. The scent of her arousal, the feel of her sweet ass on his lips and tongue, her moans, they had set him off. Too many sensations for one man to endure.

Daniel pulled himself up to a standing position behind her and let his fingers slip out of her. He undid his jeans and pulled down the zipper, wedging his pants to his thighs. His boxers followed. Then he pulled out a condom from his pocket and sheathed himself quickly.

"Can't wait any longer, baby." He tilted her toward the front and aligned his shaft with her pussy. "Gotta have you now."

One powerful thrust, and he was buried inside her.

"Oh, yes," he heard her whisper. Good, he hadn't hurt her with his impatience.

"I would have loved to throw you onto that kitchen table and flatten the pizza dough with your body."

"I think they would have thrown us out."

"Mmm, hmm." Daniel pulled himself out and plunged back into her. And again. His thrusts powered into her, one after the other as he held onto her hips to prevent her from moving. She braced herself against the railing to receive him without crumbling.

Daniel watched his shaft slide back and forth between her legs. The warmth of her body and the slickness of her flesh engulfed him.

"Baby, I can't stop."

"Then don't."

Her silken voice in his ears added to his excitement. He was out in the open, under the stars and plunging himself into the sexiest woman he'd ever met. Nothing could get better than this. Daniel didn't care if anybody saw them. If they did, they'd be envious of him for being allowed to make such a beautiful woman his own.

Her body fit so perfectly to his, and the way her muscles squeezed him so tightly inside her, drove him insane with pleasure. His hand went to the contours of her perfect ass and stroked her.

"Daniel."

Hearing her whisper his name did him in. No longer could he hold back his release. He had been hovering right at the blade's edge, but now he stepped over it, or rather jumped over it. He was heading for the abyss, and there was no better feeling than letting himself fall. His body buckled, and his climax rocked through him like powerful currents of electricity, igniting every cell in his body on the way to releasing his seed.

Breathing heavily, Daniel hugged her tightly to his body. He didn't want to leave her body, which felt like a sanctuary to him.

"I'm sorry, Holly. I'm so sorry." He knew she hadn't come, but he hadn't been able to hold on any longer. He was incensed with himself.

"Sorry about what?" She seemed oblivious to his torment.

He pulled himself out of her, shed the condom and quickly pulled his boxers and jeans up before turning her and pulling her back into his arms.

"I was selfish."

Daniel picked her up and carried her to the bench. When he lowered himself onto it to sit, he kept her in his lap. "Now it's your turn." His hand tunneled underneath her dress, stroking along her inner thigh.

***

"You don't have to do this." She was his escort, not his girlfriend. There was no need for him to satisfy her sexually. Sabrina stopped his hands from moving any further up her thigh.

He gave her a serious look. "Okay, Holly. Spit it out. Why is it that you don't want me to pleasure you? I thought you liked it."

Daniel definitely looked like he was annoyed with her. Oh, damn. She was screwing up again. "You hired me so that I can please you, not the other way around."

"Is there a rule that I'm not allowed to please you? Is the agency telling you that you can't enjoy yourself with me?" His eyes were piercing.

"No, but—"

"I paid for your time with me. But that also means I say what we do. And if I decide I'll spend my time pleasuring you, then that's what we're going to do. And if all I want is to give you orgasm after orgasm, are you going to stop me?"

"But—"

"But, what? You don't like the feeling of being touched? You don't like my hands on you?"

Sabrina knew he was provoking her, and it worked. "No. I do like it."

"Then what?"

"You reduce me to putty. I can't think straight when you touch me." Was she giving too much away? Maybe she should have kept her mouth shut. She was making herself vulnerable.

"Then don't think. Feel. That's all I want you to do. Do you have any idea what a turn on it is for a man to know he can drive a woman to ecstasy? Believe me, I get off every time I touch you. Right now, I'm hornier than I've ever been in my life."

She released his hand she'd held captured on her thigh. "I want you."

"Good, 'cause that's what you'll get. And we're not leaving here until you're completely satisfied, and I'll decide when you're truly satisfied." And his hand continued the path she had so rudely interrupted minutes earlier.

Chapter Five

They weren't alone in the elevator as they rode up to his floor. Daniel stood behind Sabrina. She eyed the older couple, who was staring straight at the elevator door in front of her, their backs to them, when she felt his head close to her ear.

"Do you want to know how hard I am, knowing that you're not wearing any panties?" he whispered into her ear before he kissed her sensitive neck.

She had to pull her handkerchief out of her bag and pretend to blow her nose in order to stifle her laughter. Not only was Daniel trying to make her lose her composure and embarrass her in front of the other couple, he had the audacity to slide his hand onto her backside and stroke her seductively through the fabric of her dress. Without her panties, it felt as if he was stroking her naked skin.

But evidently that wasn't enough for him. Sabrina felt how his hand gathered the fabric of her dress and slowly pulled it up. A whiff of cold air grazed her bare backside before she felt him press his groin into her. His erection was impossible to ignore.

Any minute now, she'd moan uncontrollably and hide in the hole that would open up in front of her. She was saved by the elevator stopping at the other couple's floor. As soon as the door closed behind them, she turned to him.

"What the hell do you think you were doing?"

Daniel laughed out loud. "Just teasing you, baby. I wanted to prove that I wasn't lying."

He took her hand and placed it on the erection straining against the zipper of his jeans. She eagerly ran her fingers up and down its length— its very impressive length.

"Can I taste that?" she asked suggestively and batted her long lashes at him as she pressed her hand harder against his erection.

He groaned loudly. "Oh, God, yes."

The more time she spent with him, the more daring she became—as if it was addictive. The thought that she would ever be in an elevator and suggest to a man that she'd suck his cock, would have horrified her two days ago. Of course, in the bedroom she'd given blowjobs before, but to suggest one in a non-bedroom environment was entirely different. It wasn't something she'd normally talk about, much less do.

But to excite him with some dirty talk suddenly turned her on.

"I can't wait to wrap my lips around you and lick you with my tongue and suck you until you come." Oh my God, she'd turned into Holly, or who was this wanton creature, who'd taken over her body and mind? "And I'm going to keep you in my mouth until you're completely spent and beg me for mercy."

Daniel pushed her against the wall and pressed his body to hers. "If you don't stop talking, I'll take you right here and won't care if anybody sees us." His eyes were dark with desire and barely leashed control.

Sabrina looked at him and licked her lips in anticipation. If he took her right here in the elevator, she wouldn't object. "Go ahead. Do it."

"God, Holly, you're killing me."

He sunk his lips onto hers and only released her when the ding of the elevator sounded as it stopped on their floor. Seconds later, he opened the door to his room, pushed her in and let it slam shut behind them.

Without a word, he pressed her against the wall and dropped down to the floor as he lifted her dress. Less than a second later, his mouth was pressed between her legs, his tongue licking her pussy, lapping up the moisture that oozed from her. He licked her as if he were starving, moaning into her body.

"Daniel, how come you never do that to me?" a female voice pulled Sabrina out of her bliss. Daniel let go of her instantaneously and jolted upright. They both gaped at the beautiful redhead, who stood in the door to the bedroom, dressed in a revealing negligee. She leaned seductively at the door frame.

"Audrey, what the f—" Daniel sounded furious.

Realization flushed through Sabrina. He knew her. His wife? Fiancée? Girlfriend? Why had she assumed he was unattached? This couldn't be happening. This was her worst nightmare playing out right in front of her.

"Well, that's what I could say. I leave you alone for a couple of days, and look what happens." Her voice was sugary sweet.

"Audrey, how did you get in here?"

"You forget that my name was on the reservation. I came to talk to you."

"We have nothing to talk about." With every word, his voice became angrier and more booming as if he was barely able to keep his temper in check.

Sabrina backed away and reached for the door. "I'd better go."

She first thought nobody had heard her and pushed down the handle, but Daniel jerked around to her.

"No, Holly, you're staying. Audrey is leaving." His voice was commanding.

"I can't," Sabrina pressed out and ran out the door.

"Holly, come back," Daniel's voice roared behind her, but she ran for the elevator, which opened miraculously. The doors closed before he could reach her.

In the lobby, she didn't care that the staff gave her strange looks when she ran out the door. She had to get away. She wasn't Holly, and she wasn't made for this. She had promised herself that she wouldn't get hurt, but she knew she had. She had to leave before it got any worse.

Daniel was just another man out for some amusement, cheating on his wife or girlfriend. He'd probably lied to her when he'd said he'd never been with an escort. Most likely, he did this on every business trip.

How could she have let her guard down and trusted him with her body the way she had? And what was even worse: with her heart. Her emotions had been along for the ride, all the way. She should have never given into Holly and substituted for her. This wasn't her world, and now she had the wounds to show for it.

When Sabrina reached her apartment, she ran into her room and shut the door before she allowed the tears to run down her face. Holly knew her well enough to leave her alone until she was ready to talk. This time she wouldn't talk. She couldn't tell anybody about the shame she felt or the hurt in her heart.

Why had she let this happen? She should have quit while she was ahead. After the first night with him, she should have never gone back. She felt like a gambler in Las Vegas who'd won big the first night and then gone back to put all her chips on the table the next night and lost it all.

She'd let her guard down and allowed him to come close, not just sexually, but more so emotionally. Maybe there wouldn't be the embarrassment this time since she'd never see him again, but it didn't diminish the pain she felt. This hurt more than what had happened to her in law school.

It was a relief when sleep finally claimed her and stopped her mind from clicking.

***

Daniel's night wasn't quite over yet. Audrey was in hysterics. When she'd realized that her seduction efforts didn't pay off, she'd tried the tearful route. This time it wouldn't work on him. She might as well talk to a stone statue.

"I'm not listening to any more of this. It's time for you to leave." He'd had it with her. She'd completely destroyed his perfect evening with Holly and caused her to run out on him. He wanted nothing more to do with Audrey.

"What does this little tramp have that I don't?" she provoked him.

Daniel gave her an angry glare. "She's not a tramp!"

"She must be. This is your third night here, and already she's sleeping with you. Only a whore would do that!"

"Who the hell are you, calling her a whore? Are you any better? No, your price is just higher. But you spread your legs for a man just as quickly if he's got enough money or prestige and you think you can get him to marry you. Don't think you can stay on your high horse and look down on other women."

The shocked look on her face told him she hadn't expected his reaction.

"So don't you call her a whore! She's got more honesty in her little finger than you can muster in your entire body. And yes, I've been sleeping with her. And I've never had better sex in my entire life. And I'm going to go right back to her. You and I were over the minute you jumped into bed with Judd. Go right back to him, and see if he can make you happy. 'Cause I'm not interested."

By now he was fuming. Not only did it hit close to home when she'd called Holly a whore, but in that instant he'd realized that he didn't care if she was a whore or not, he just cared about having her back in his arms. At least, Holly was honest about selling herself, which was more than could be said for those society whores, who pretended to be so high and mighty but sold themselves for another currency: power, prestige, and a rich husband.

"Get out!" Daniel snapped, and Audrey finally seemed to see the rage in him. Yes, she should fear him, because if she kept him from Holly any longer, he'd forget his good upbringing and toss her out of his room without the benefit of clothes other than the ones she wore at present.

Less than a minute later, she'd grabbed her suitcase, thrown a coat over her negligee and stomped through the door he held open for her. He'd never seen her act this quickly on anything.

"You'll regret this, and then you'll beg me to come back to you," she hissed.

Daniel shook his head. "Don't hold your breath. I can guarantee you, you'll suffocate."

He let the door slam behind her. It was the best sound he'd heard in the last half hour.

On his Blackberry, he found the number for the agency and dialed it. He needed to get in touch with Holly.

A female voice answered. "Good evening." No name.

"Yes, I'm trying to get in touch with one of your employees. We accidentally got separated this evening, and I need to ... I need to contact her to give her my whereabouts." He hoped it sounded believable enough.

"I'm sorry, Sir, but it's company policy not to give out our employees' contact information. It's for their protection, I'm sure you'll understand." She was friendly enough but firm.

"But this is really an emergency. As I said, we got separated, and our evening isn't over yet."

He needed to see her.

"I'm sorry, sir," she repeated in the same tone. "I can take a message and pass it on to her tomorrow morning."

"Tomorrow morning?" Unacceptable. Too late.

"Yes, sir. We don't contact our employees after midnight."

"Forget it."

He disconnected the call. Damn Audrey! He could be in bed with

Holly now, having the most amazing sex of his life, and instead, here he stood, angry, frustrated and without a means to contact her.

Handsome Adonis seeks Goddess of Love.

Where was she, his love goddess? Why had she run off? Maybe it was company policy to avoid fights with clients' spouses or girlfriends. It was probably survival instinct for any escort not to get between a client and his angry other half.

Hell, if he'd only known how to get in contact with her, then they could continue where they'd left off. His body was yearning for her. Her taste was still on his tongue, and he hadn't had nearly enough of her. He couldn't explain it to himself, and he didn't want to analyze it, but he knew he wanted her. And by God, he'd have her.

The way she'd felt in his arms when he'd made her come on the bench, and how she'd kissed him after that, wasn't something anybody could buy. No, what she'd given him wasn't for sale. The way she'd kissed him wasn't because he was paying for it. He was convinced of it. Holly wanted him too. It had to be. It just had to be that way.

***

Sabrina had a hard time getting up and would have liked to call in sick, but then she would have moped around the flat all day long and just cried some more. She knew it was better not to allow herself to sink any deeper into her sorrow and pull herself up. She had to pretend that everything was okay, even though she knew it wasn't.

Despite what she'd promised herself, she'd gotten hurt. She'd fallen hard for Daniel. When it had happened, she wasn't quite sure. Maybe during the cooking class when they'd kneaded the dough together, or maybe when he'd turned into a rascal and they'd trespassed. It didn't matter when it had happened, just that it had.

And he wasn't worthy of her emotions. Daniel was a cheating, lying son of a bitch, not any better than the guy she'd slept with in law school. How could he? And all this time, he'd been so sweet to her, so caring. It made him even more of a cad.

No, she had to forget about him. He wasn't worth it. She had to move on. And nobody could know about it, not even Holly. If Holly found out that she'd fallen in love with him, she'd blame herself. And it wasn't Holly's fault. It was hers.

Sabrina poured herself a quick cup of coffee and drank it standing in the kitchen. She wanted to avoid her roommate and get into work early, but she wasn't lucky. Holly had obviously heard her and gotten up despite the fact that it was far too early for her. Holly never got up before ten in the morning.

"What happened last night?" Holly needed no preliminaries when she wanted to get to the bottom of things.

Sabrina avoided her gaze. "Nothing. Everything's fine. I have to be at work early. Big case."

She put her coffee mug down on the counter and snatched her briefcase.

"Sabrina, please," Holly insisted.

"It's fine." She rushed out and let the door close behind her.

She had no big case to attend to. Nothing particularly important was waiting for her at work. But at least she could busy herself and make the day go by faster. When she arrived at work, the place was already buzzing like a beehive.

"What's going on, Caroline?" she asked the receptionist. "Why's everybody in so early?"

"Haven't you heard? We picked up some really big client from the East Coast. He's coming for a meeting in an hour."

Sabrina shrugged. Nobody ever told her anything, and obviously she wasn't going to be working on the new client's case anyway, especially not if he was a really big client, as Caroline had put it. Nobody ever gave her any important assignments.

She opened the door to her tiny office and buried herself in boring depositions, which needed reviewing. Everybody left her alone. It appeared everybody but she was assigned to the new client. Perfect. Her love life was a mess, and her career was going nowhere.

Her intercom buzzed. "Hannigan wants a copy of the Fleming depositions. Do you have those, Sabrina?" Caroline's voice came through.

"I've just finished reviewing them. You can pick them up and copy them for him."

"Sorry, can't. I'm not allowed to leave the reception desk today."

"Then have Helen do it."

"Helen is working on something for the new client. I'm sorry, but there's nobody else to copy those. And Hannigan wants them now."

Sabrina sighed. "Fine. I'll do it myself." Now she was even relegated to secretarial duties. Great! The day was getting better by the minute. What else was there that could go wrong?

She passed the conference room on her way to the copier room. The conference room was on one end of their floor and had glass walls. When they'd remodeled the office, the partners had insisted on something grand to impress the clients. The conference room looked out over the city, and the glass wall between the room and the foyer added to the impressive view.

All partners, several associates and other men Sabrina couldn't quite make out were huddled over the conference table talking loudly amongst themselves and passing documents between them. A bunch of suits. In the end, they all looked the same. Not a single woman among them.

She entered the copier room and punched in her code to start copying the depositions. The machine made a loud humming noise as it started its job. Bored, she tapped her fingers on the control panel.

"Waiting for something?" a voice coming from the door startled her.

She turned in lightning speed and saw how Hannigan closed the door behind him and locked it from the inside. Instantly, cold sweat broke out on her skin. Oh God, he'd tricked her. He'd sent her to do the copying job knowing that none of the secretaries was available, so he could trap her in here.

Sabrina's stomach turned, and she felt sick.

"I'm almost done here. I can bring the papers to your office." She tried to remain calm and pretend she didn't know what he was up to.

"That won't be necessary." His disgusting tongue snaked out and licked his lips.

She felt bile rise. There was only one exit to this room, and Hannigan was blocking it.

"It's much cozier here anyway. What do you say, Sabrina?"

He made a step toward her, and she jerked back.

"Mr. Hannigan, I'll bring the papers to your office." She tried to be as formal as possible to tell him that he wasn't welcome.

"Come on, Sabrina, I'm sure under this cool exterior there's a whole lot of passion buried." He was only too right, but the passion in her wasn't meant for him, not even if he were the last men on earth and the future of the world depended on them procreating.

"Mr. Hannigan, I have to ask you to let me pass. I have work to do." She tried to keep the shaking of her voice under control. She couldn't show him how scared she was.

"I'll tell you where your work is. It's right here." He grabbed his crotch.

"Mr. Hannigan, I have to ask you to stop this, or I'll—"

"Or you'll what? Tell the partners?" He laughed. "They're not going to touch me, trust me."

He took another step toward her. Sabrina backed up against a stack of paper. To her left was the copier machine, which was too bulky for her to get around, and to her right were several cases of paper, but stacked only one foot high. It would be easy to step over them.

"Sabrina, I can make your work here easy or hard. You choose."

She had the feeling he wasn't here to give her a choice. He was here to force his choice on her. His position was pretty clear from where she stood. Either she gave into his demands, or he'd force himself on her. No, she couldn't let this happen. She had to get out of here before he laid as much as a finger on her.

Sabrina sized up the situation quickly. In order for her to get behind him to unlock the door, she'd have to let him get closer. It was risky and not only that: the thought of having him come any closer was disgusting and made her want to puke.

But it had to be done. Eying the door behind him, she forced a smile on her lips. Hopefully, she'd learned enough from Holly to know how to trick him into thinking he'd get his way with her. She saw him relax when he noticed her smile. Slowly, Hannigan made another step toward her. Now was the time to act.

Chapter Six

Daniel stared out the window of the conference room at the Law Offices of Brand, Freeman & Merriweather. Behind him, the lawyers discussed the best way to handle the contingency that was holding up the deal. He'd lost interest in the discussions half an hour ago, and his mind had drifted back to Holly. Before he'd met her, he'd never had any trouble keeping his mind squarely focused on business. It was different this time.

He suddenly didn't care much about the deal he'd worked on for over a year. The thought that he had to sit through countless other meetings like this one in the next few days made him feel exhausted and weary.

"Mr. Sinclair, how about we ask them for a one million dollar bond to be released only if the contingency is met by our extended due date?" Mr. Merriweather suggested.

Daniel turned to consider the proposition and froze. His eyes had drifted toward the reception area. Holly—*his Holly!*—walked through one of the office doors into the foyer and crossed it hastily. She looked different. She wore a business suit, but her hair was disheveled and the collar of her blouse was out of place. As she disappeared through another door, his gaze was suddenly drawn back to the door she'd exited from. It opened again, and a man in his forties came out. He glanced to each side as if he didn't want to be noticed while he tucked his tie back into his suit and adjusted his jacket. His face appeared flushed.

Damn! Oh, God, no! This couldn't be happening. Holly was here to service another client.

"Mr. Sinclair?" Merriweather reminded him that he was still waiting for an answer.

"Sure, let's do that. Why don't I leave you to work out the details? You know my sentiments. Gentlemen, you know what to do," he excused himself.

Daniel hurried out of the room, eager to catch Holly. The thought that she'd been with another man was as if a wire hanger was slowly being pushed through his guts. Excruciatingly slowly. Damn, if he'd let some other man touch her!

His search for her was fruitless. The door he'd seen her leave through went straight to the stairs, and by the time he'd reached the bottom and gotten outside, she was nowhere to be seen. She obviously knew how to make a quick escape, not that she'd seen him, but she probably knew how to get away unseen in case the office staff had noticed anything going on.

His hands balled into fists as he recalled the face of the man who'd come out of the room after her. The thought of that pig's hands on her made him want to kick somebody, preferably that pig. He had to draw on all his self control not to go back up to the office and pummel that bastard's face with his fists until his face was bloody mush.

Daniel pulled out his cell phone and dialed.

"Good morning," a friendly female voice chirped.

"Miss Snyder, please. Daniel Sinclair."

He was connected instantly. "Mr. Sinclair, how may I help you?"

"I'd like to book Holly."

"Certainly. What time slot?"

"Exclusively starting from today through the entire next week. She's not to have any other clients," he barked into the phone.

"Mr. Sinclair. This is highly unusual. I believe it would be better if we discussed this in my office."

"Fine."

"I can see you at 2 p.m. My assistant will give you instructions on how to get here."

She transferred him back to the girl, who'd answered the phone. After she gave him the address, he cut her off.

"I know where it is."

Daniel didn't care that he sounded rude. He was in no mood to be polite. He knew exactly what the feeling in his gut was, but he wasn't ready to acknowledge it. It was better not to think of it.

He headed for a dive and ordered a stiff drink at the bar. He had over two hours to kill, and while he was sure Tim would have loved to have lunch with him, he wasn't sure he could face his all too perceptive friend right now. He'd see right through him and call him on it. And then what? He'd have to admit to himself what had happened. No, he wasn't quite ready for that.

It was easier to kick back a couple of drinks at a bar and pretend to watch sports on the TV that hung over it. Right now, he was all for doing the easy thing. It would get much harder later.

The bartender gave him a look as if he knew what was going on inside his head. "You want nuts with that?"

"Sure." He hadn't had any lunch, and he wasn't hungry, so nuts were as good a choice as any.

As the bartender shoved the bowl of nuts in front of him, Daniel only nodded.

"Can't live with them, can't live without them," the bartender suddenly said.

"Do I look like I want to listen to some clichés?" he snorted.

"Not really, but at least it got you talking."

"Who says I want to talk?"

"Midday, alone in a bar, hard liquor. Yeah, you're here for a talk. Seen the type."

"What is it with you guys? Do you all have degrees in psychology?" Irritated, Daniel sniffed.

"Personally I don't, but I can't speak for the rest of my colleagues. So, what's she done?" he asked casually while taking out a tray of wet glasses from the dishwasher.

"Who we're talking about?"

"The woman who's driving you into a bar at midday."

God, that bartender was one pain in the ass. Maybe he should just finish his drink and leave. There had to be another bar somewhere nearby with a less irritating bartender.

"Why does there have to be a woman if a man wants to have a drink?" He wasn't going to cave in that easily.

"There's always a woman. That's what makes us tick." The words of wisdom just rolled off his tongue like a penny down a steep street—and just as valuable, Daniel was sure.

He was ready to bite back with sarcasm but thought better of it. There was no need to waste his energy. "So what?"

"So, she doesn't want you. Is that it?"

"Has nobody ever told you how unwelcome your advice is?" Daniel kicked back the rest of his drink and stood. "Here." He put a bill on the counter, not bothering to wait for his change. "And just so you know, she *does* want me. And I'm going to make her realize that."

Daniel strolled through the streets until it was time to meet with Misty Snyder, the owner of the escort service, or rather the Madam. As soon as he entered the elegant but sparse office, he knew she ran a tight ship. The receptionist was dressed in a conservative business suit and wore minimal makeup. There was a waiting area and several private offices.

Nothing gave away the fact that these were the offices of an escort service. There was nothing smutty about it. If anybody saw him in the waiting area, they would think he was here to meet his accountant.

Frankly, he had expected something different, some frills, something over the top, not the neat and clean office he was impatiently waiting in.

"Mr. Sinclair," a middle-aged woman greeted him and shook his hand. She was dressed in an equally conservative business suit as her receptionist and wore her hair in a loose bun. She was attractive and gave him a charming smile.

"Ms. Snyder."

"Eva, show Holly into the conference room as soon as she arrives," she instructed her receptionist before she directed him toward one of the doors. "Please."

"Holly is coming here?" Daniel asked as soon as the door closed behind them.

"Yes, I find it prudent to discuss such lengthy bookings with my employees. We don't want there to be any misunderstandings later." She gave him a serious look.

"That's very wise."

"Especially given your request of exclusivity, I feel that Holly needs to agree to all terms. Don't you think so?"

Daniel could tell she was curious why he required exclusivity, but he wouldn't say more than he absolutely had to in order to strike the deal. He was an experienced negotiator and knew not to show his hand. "I agree."

"You'll of course understand that the daily cost for such a booking will be higher than what you've been paying for her evenings. Since we won't be able to charge her out during the day, we'll have to factor this in."

Misty was a shrewd business woman, he could tell. She was already positioning herself so she could get the best price from him. If she only knew that money was no object when it came to Holly.

The truth was he didn't care if she charged him five times the going rate, as long as it guaranteed that he could be with Holly and no other man laid a hand on her. And the sooner this happened, the better.

"There'll of course also be a cancellation fee should you decide to terminate early." Misty searched his face for any objection to her suggestion, but found none. There'd be no early termination. By the time the end of the week rolled around, he'd have Holly right where he wanted her, and—

The door opened, interrupting his thoughts when a young blonde woman stepped in.

"Eva said to come right in, sorry."

Misty waived her in and pointed to a chair. "Sit down, Holly. I'm just going over the terms and conditions with Mr. Sinclair."

Holly? Daniel jerked and stared at the woman. This wasn't Holly. This had to be a mistake. This wasn't *his* Holly. The blonde woman looked directly at him as if she wanted to tell him something, but she didn't say another word.

Realizing something was fishy, he addressed the Madam. "Ms. Snyder, would you mind if I talked to Holly privately for a few minutes?"

Misty raised her eyebrows and seemed to debate whether it was safe to leave them alone. "I'll be right outside."

"Thank you."

As soon as the door shut behind her, Daniel turned back to the blonde woman.

"Who the hell are you, and where is the real Holly?"

"I am the real Holly," she insisted.

"Listen, I don't know what kind of bait and switch operation this is, but don't take me for a fool. I've spent the last two nights with Holly, and that's the Holly I want." His tone was determined. If they tried to play him, he'd make sure they'd be sorry later.

The blonde pressed her eyelids together quickly, then looked back at him. "God, I had no idea this would happen. I was sick that night I was booked to see you, so I had somebody fill in for me. Misty doesn't know."

A sense of relief flooded through him. "No problem. Just tell me what her name is, and I'll book her. No offense." He'd have to get used to calling her a different name, but that was the least of his problems.

"Well, that's a problem."

"That's not a problem. I'll just tell your boss that I changed my mind and then book your colleague."

Holly shifted uncomfortably on her chair. She nervously flicked her hair back over her shoulder. "She isn't a colleague."

"You mean she's from a different agency?" Daniel was getting impatient. He didn't want to waste his time here. Every minute he was separated from *his* Holly meant some slimy guy could get his hands on her.

"Who is she? Do you want me to call Ms. Snyder in here?" If he had to threaten her, he would.

Holly held up her hand to stop him. "I'm sorry, I can't tell you."

Daniel got up. "I'd better discuss this with your boss."

"She's my roommate. She's not an escort," Holly stopped him.

The implications of her words didn't immediately register with him. *Her roommate. Not an escort.* He fell back onto the chair.

"Hold it! What did you say?"

"She's my roommate."

"No. Not that."

"She's not an escort."

"But …" He stopped. "But she was with me. The last two nights."

"Because I was sick," Holly explained. "Misty would have fired me if I hadn't taken the booking, so I talked her into it."

God, his Holly wasn't an escort. "She's not an escort. She's a real person?"

"Thanks a lot!"

"Sorry, didn't mean it. She's not an escort. She's … What's her real name?"

"Sabrina."

"Sabrina." He let it roll off his tongue and immediately knew it suited her so much better. Then he suddenly remembered the incident at the law offices.

"If she's not an escort, what the hell was she doing with that pig at the office?" Daniel was angry just thinking about it.

"What pig at what office?"

"Brand, Freeman & Merriweather. She was there this morning and came out of somebody's office all ruffled." He gave Holly a questioning look.

"The pig you're referring to is Hannigan. He's been harassing her ever since she started working there."

Anger flared up from his gut, and he slammed his fist on the table. "I'll kick the shit out of that bastard."

"Get in line. I've got first dibs on that asshole."

Daniel settled back into his chair. It pleased him that Sabrina had a friend, who was willing to go to bat for her. He gave her a smile. "She works there?"

Holly nodded. "She's an attorney."

Now it dawned on him. At the reception she'd simply reverted to being herself. No wonder she'd been able to handle Bob.

"Hastings Law School?"

"How did you know?"

"She mentioned it at the reception I took her to. I thought she'd trip herself up. I guess I didn't have to worry." He paused, now serious. "Holly, tell me what's going on. I don't understand why she did it."

"Why? I'm very persuasive. She knew what was at stake for me. I just wish I would have never asked her to do it." She gave him a serious look of her own.

"What do you mean? She wasn't with anybody else but me, was she? Has she done this before?" Anger boiled up in him again. If somebody else had touched her, he'd be ready to kill him.

"No! It was just you. So *you* tell me something now. Why the hell was she crying her eyes out last night? What did you do to her?" Holly moved forward to emphasize that she wanted an answer.

"She cried? Oh God, I'm an idiot." Daniel raked his hands through his hair.

"Hey, I'll be the first one to agree with you if you give me more details." Holly sat back, clearly getting ready for a juicy story.

"Last night my ex-girlfriend showed up at the hotel," he explained.

"Oh, boy. That's not a good start."

"It didn't end well either. I think Holly ... sorry, Sabrina thought I was cheating on my girlfriend with her. She didn't know that Audrey is my ex. She just showed up thinking she can have me back." He winced at the memory. Now he understood why Sabrina had run. It wasn't some company policy to get out of the firing line between couples. She'd left because she felt betrayed by him.

"And, are you taking her back?" Holly wanted to know.

"Audrey? Not in a million years. The woman is completely shallow and self-absorbed. Unfortunately, she managed to make Sabrina think I was still with her. So she ran off. And I haven't been able to get in touch with her since. I called the office last night after she left, but they wouldn't give me any information." He paused and looked straight at her. "You have to help me."

"Help you with what?"

"I want Sabrina back." It was straight forward. He wanted her.

"Excuse me, but didn't you hear what I said earlier? She's *not* an escort."

Daniel gripped Holly's forearms and made her look at him. "Holly, I want Sabrina back. I need her."

"Are you crazy? She's not for sale. You can't just book her." She shook her head and pulled out of his grip. "What the hell do you want from her?"

He couldn't answer that question, not if he didn't want to admit to himself why he wanted her and why he got angry every time he thought of another man touching her.

"I need to tell her the truth about Audrey. I don't want her to think I'm some cheating son-of-a-bitch. Please, you have to tell me, where I can find her."

"And let her know that you know she's not an escort?"

"Excuse me? Of course. I'll clear everything up with her."

"The hell you will!"

Was this woman crazy? What reason could she possibly have for not telling Sabrina the truth?

"If she finds out that you know she's not an escort, she'll be horrified."

"Horrified?" He had no idea what Holly was talking about.

"She doesn't trust men, because too many assholes treated her badly. Before you, she hadn't had sex in three years. Now I finally get her to let go of her inhibitions, and you're going to destroy it all by telling her you know she's not an escort. Fabulous!" Holly huffed indignantly.

"Why would that destroy anything?"

"Because she only slept with you because she thought she'd never see you again, so you couldn't hurt her. And besides, she felt safe because she could pretend to be somebody else. She could pretend it wasn't *her* having sex with a stranger. She could pretend it was *me*."

And then it dawned on him. "You planned this?" Startled, he looked at her.

"It took me long enough. I had to wait for the right man for her."

Her admission shocked him. What kind of person would knowingly send her friend into the lion's den?

"You couldn't have known that I'd be the right man. You could have sent her in with some pervert. Are you crazy?" Daniel was furious.

Holly sighed impatiently. "Do you really think we're amateurs? We get bios and detailed background checks on anybody who books us. Trust me, we know who we're dealing with. Why do you think you pay through the nose for our time? All that background work has to be paid for somehow."

"You knew who I was?"

She nodded. "Pictures, birth date, social security number, birthmarks, family background, gossip, jobs, investments. When I saw your picture I knew she'd like you. Hell, I would have done you, but—"

"—you were sick that night," he sarcastically completed her sentence.

"No. I have the constitution of a horse. I took some stuff to make myself throw up so it would look realistic. Otherwise she would have smelled a rat. So, there's no way you're going to tell her now that you know she's not an escort. She's not ready for that."

Holly crossed her arms in front of her chest, a sure sign that she wasn't going to budge.

"Fine. For now. But I'm not going to let her continue thinking I lied to her about Audrey. I'm going to fix this. So you, Holly, will help me just the same. I'll book Holly for the next week, and *you* will make sure *she* will take the booking."

"You can't be serious!"

"Oh, I'm dead serious. You'll tell her today that as of tomorrow morning she's with me."

"She's never going to agree. She thinks you lied to her. She's hurt."

He wouldn't be dissuaded. "That's why you're going to give her my cell number and have her call me tonight." He wrote his number on a card and handed it to her. "Tell her whatever you have to. Tell her if she doesn't want to take the booking, she'll have to convince me to cancel with your boss, otherwise you get fired. I need to speak to her."

Reluctantly, Holly put his card into her bag. "Had I known how stubborn you are, I would have never asked her to do this."

"You know what, Holly? If it had been you that night, I would have never had sex with you. No offense, you're a gorgeous woman, but I wasn't looking for sex that night. I just needed somebody to fend off those single women at the reception. But when I saw her, everything changed. And I'm not just going to let her go."

"Remind me again why I'm helping you."

"Because you love your friend," he responded simply. "And because I could still get you fired if I told your boss."

Daniel got up. "I will pay the entire exorbitant fee your boss suggests since we don't want anybody to smell a rat. Whether you give the money to Sabrina or not, doesn't matter to me."

"She didn't take the money for the first two nights. Flat out refused it," Holly admitted.

He smiled and relaxed. "I figured as much." She hadn't taken his tip either, and the thought of it pleased him now that he knew who she was. If Sabrina needed to pretend she was an escort in order to be with him, he'd play along—for now. Until he could figure out a way for her to trust him enough to be with him because she wanted to and not because he paid for it.

"Hey, buddy. One more thing: if you hurt her, I'm coming after you to kick the living daylights out of you." Holly gave him a firm stare.

Daniel nodded. "I wouldn't expect anything less."

Chapter Seven

"No, I'm not doing this again," Sabrina announced angrily. "I've had enough. You'll just have to go to Misty and tell her." She stormed into her room and slammed the door shut behind her. Seconds later, it opened again.

"I can't. She'll fire me," Holly retorted as she stepped into the room. "The only way we can get out of it is if you can make him cancel the booking from his side."

"And how am I going to do that?"

Holly handed her a card with a number. "Call him, and tell him you can't do it. Tell him you find him disgusting, whatever it takes to make him cancel."

"I don't want to talk to him!"

"Well, I'm afraid that's the only way this is going to work."

Sabrina stared at her friend. She didn't understand why Holly couldn't be more supporting. After all, she'd helped her out of a jam, and at least she could be more understanding about her refusal to see Daniel again. She could make up any excuse with Misty to get out of the booking, but she flat out refused to do just that.

Instead, Holly insisted that Daniel was the one who cancelled so she would be out of trouble. Perfect.

Sabrina didn't know why Daniel still wanted to see her. Hadn't his wife or girlfriend gotten back last night? How had he managed to get rid of her that quickly? Lying, cheating bastard!

She felt like sinking into the ground for shame about what they'd done the night before. She'd let him use her. Jerk! The gall he had to request her for a long-term booking after all he'd done. Cad!

She was in the right mood to tell him just what she thought of him! Self-righteous philanderer!

Sabrina grabbed the phone off the hook then gave her friend a sharp look. "Can I get some privacy here?" she barked.

Holly instantly shuffled out of the room.

The line was picked up instantly.

"This is Daniel." His voice was as smooth as it had been the night before.

"It's S … Holly."

"I'm glad you're calling."

"I'm only calling to tell you that I can't take the booking." She kept her voice tight. "So, if you'd please call Ms. Snyder to cancel, I'd appreciate it."

"I think we should talk about this."

"There's nothing to talk about."

"There is. Why did you run out on me yesterday?"

Sabrina exhaled sharply. "Why? I don't come between couples. I might be an escort, but I have my standards."

"I'm not with Audrey anymore."

"Well, maybe not at this moment, but you are with her, she made that pretty clear."

"Holly, Audrey and I broke up before I left New York. She just couldn't face the truth. Please let me explain. Please. Meet me tonight, and I'll explain everything to you, and if you then still want me to cancel then, I will."

"I'm not that stupid. As soon as I'm in your room, you'll just haul me off to bed, and there won't be any talking. No thanks."

"Meet me at a coffee shop. Please. I promise, if after our meeting you want me to cancel, I will."

Sabrina was torn. She knew nothing good could come from meeting him, but she could also sense the determination in his voice. He wouldn't agree to a cancellation if he didn't get a chance to give his side of the events.

"Okay."

She gave him directions to a coffee shop in her neighborhood and hung up. She should be whipped for agreeing to see him.

Sabrina had chosen the coffee shop around the corner because it was always busy. There'd be no chance he could pull a fast one on her there. And it certainly wasn't an intimate place. There was no place to hide, no dark corners or niches where he could ply her with his charm.

She would arrive early to stake out the least private area in the coffee shop. She wasn't going to make this pleasant for him. If he thought he could use his sexy body to change her mind, he'd have another thought coming.

Unfortunately, it turned out that his sexy body came with an extremely sharp mind that had already anticipated her move. As soon as she arrived at the coffee shop, ten minutes early, she saw him. Daniel had managed to snap up the only couch in the place. How he'd done it, she had no idea, since the couch was permanently occupied by somebody or other.

He stood up and waved at her. Grudgingly, she walked toward him.

"I see you're early too." He smiled knowingly and pointed to the spot on the two-seater couch next to him. As they sat, she was too aware of his body and his male scent permeating the air.

"Thanks for coming." He gave her a sincere look. "I'm sorry for what happened last night."

"Which part?" she shot back.

"Only the part when Audrey showed up. Everything else was perfect."

"Oh, I bet!"

"Would you please let me explain? Audrey and I were dating for a few months, but things weren't really going anywhere. I wasn't exactly the most attentive boyfriend or the most romantic. I guess she felt lonely, and then this week I found her in bed with my attorney. So I broke up with her."

"Does she know you broke up with her? It didn't look to me like she did," Sabrina interjected caustically.

"She knows. She just didn't want to face the truth. She figured she could get me back if she pouted long enough."

"So, did she pout long enough?" Sabrina didn't dare look at him as she asked her question. From the corner of her eye, she saw how he shook his head slowly.

"No amount of pouting will make me get back with her." Quite unexpectedly, Daniel took her hand. "You're not getting in between a couple. I'm single, I'm not in a relationship, and I'm free to do what I want." He forced her to turn toward him.

"Why me? Can't you just book somebody else? The agency has lots of nice women you can choose from."

He inched closer to her as Sabrina sank back into her corner of the couch. She tried to pull her hand away, but he didn't release her. "I feel comfortable with you. I'd like to spend more time with you."

"I don't think it's a good idea. Misty doesn't like us to get too comfortable with our clients," Sabrina lied.

"Misty didn't seem to have a problem with it when I negotiated the deal with her this afternoon." Daniel pulled her hand to his mouth and kissed it tenderly.

His kiss spread a wave of heat throughout her body. "I can't do it. Sorry. Choose somebody else. There are plenty of women who'd jump at the chance to have sex with you. But I'm not one of them."

"You're not interested in having sex with me anymore?" His eyes narrowed.

"No, I'm not." She couldn't remember ever having had a bigger lie come over her lips.

He gave her a long look. "Fine."

Good, she'd finally convinced him that she wanted nothing to do with him. Now all he needed to do was to cancel the booking, and she and Holly would be home free and out of trouble.

Sabrina shifted on the couch to get up, but his arm pulled her back down before she'd even had a chance to lift herself up.

"I said fine, no sex. But I didn't say you'll get out of the booking."

She glared at him, shocked. If he didn't want sex, why hire an escort? What was wrong with this man? "Excuse me?"

"You heard me. You'll call the shots when it comes to sex. If you don't want to sleep with me, I won't force you. But you'll come to the wine country with me this weekend. I've reserved us a little bed and breakfast for tomorrow night. And you'll share my bed. And I'm allowed to kiss you."

She was so screwed. How was she supposed to *not* want to have sex with him when he insisted on them sharing a bed?

"You're crazy."

"Be that as it may, that's my compromise, you spend the weekend with me, as well as the evenings and nights when we're back in town, and you'll sleep in my bed. I'll make no attempt to have sex with you unless you want me to."

Daniel seemed serious about the proposal. But she didn't understand him. "Why would you book an escort knowing she doesn't want to have sex with you? That's the most hare-brained idea I've ever heard."

He shrugged. "I like your company, with or without sex." He moved his head closer to hers, looking suggestively at her lips. "Maybe you should say *yes* right now, before I have to use other means of persuasion, which might not be appropriate for a neighborhood coffee shop."

Sabrina shot him a shocked look. "You wouldn't!" Would he really embarrass them both and make out with her right in the middle of the coffee shop where everybody could see them? He couldn't possible have in mind to touch her the way he'd touched her before when they were alone.

Looking at the wicked glint in his eyes, she realized he had no scruples. And knowing that he was from out of town, he probably didn't even care if he embarrassed them. *He* didn't have to come back here day after day to get his coffee. *She* did.

"Baby, you have no idea what I'm capable of."

His lips brushed lightly against hers in a barely-there kiss.

Sabrina gasped instantly. "Okay. But you have to keep your side of the bargain. No sex."

"As long as you keep to yours. You share my bed, and you'll let me kiss you."

Seconds ticked by until she finally nodded in agreement and Daniel pulled back and smiled. "I'm glad we finally agree. Even though, this could have been fun."

She cringed when she saw his wicked smile before he broke out in hearty laughter.

"Come, I'll walk you home so I know where to pick you up tomorrow morning."

"No, that's not necessary." It was better if he didn't know where she lived. "And besides, it's against company policy."

"Ms. Snyder authorized it since I'm taking you out of town tomorrow."

He took her arm and led her out of the shop.

As they arrived at her building, he took her hand into his again. "Bring some casual clothes, we'll be touring the vineyards in Sonoma. And a swimsuit. There's a pool at the place we're staying. I'll pick you up at 9am."

He kissed the palm of her hand then let it go.

"Daniel," she started.

He locked eyes with her. "What?"

She shook her head slowly. No, she couldn't tell him the truth. "Nothing. I'll see you tomorrow."

"Good night."

When she reached the flat and opened the door, Holly was waiting for her.

"And? Is he going to cancel?" she got down to the most important question immediately.

Sabrina shook her head. "No, he's picking me up tomorrow morning to go to the wine country for the weekend."

"Are you okay with that?" Holly asked softly.

"I think you should stock up on ice cream, because when he leaves and goes back to his normal life in New York, I'm going to need comfort food. A lot of comfort food. Holly, I'm so screwed."

Her friend instantly wrapped her arms around her and took her into a tight bear hug. "Is he that bad?"

Sabrina sobbed uncontrollably into her friend's shoulder. "No. He's that good," she wailed.

Holly gently stroked her hair. "Oh, sweetie, just try to enjoy the time you have with him, and maybe it'll all turn out all right."

***

Daniel had debated whether to spend the evening with Sabrina, but he didn't want to push her. He needed to tread carefully from now on. He had to make her trust him, and this would be a slow process.

Instantly dragging her back into bed with him wouldn't work, as much as he wanted to do just that. That's why he'd suggested to her that she would be the one to initiate sex. Maybe it would give her the safety net she needed. And he was willing to keep up his end of the bargain, as hard as it was for him.

He had to work on a slow seduction without her even noticing what he was doing. Holly was right, Sabrina could be easily scared away if she found out too early that her whole charade had already been discovered. She felt safe now, pretending to be somebody else, but how would she react when she knew her cover was blown? The only way to make her safe after that was to replace her cover with trust.

Daniel sat across from Tim during dinner at a small neighborhood restaurant.

"Let me get this straight. You want to romance an escort?" Tim grinned from one ear to the other.

"As I've already told you, she's not a real escort," he pointedly corrected his friend.

"Semantics. Nevertheless, she slept with you for money." Tim was clearly having fun needling him and would continue as long as he could get away with it.

"She didn't take the money, her friend did."

"So she slept with you because ...? Help me out here, Danny."

He frowned. "What? You think I can't attract a woman without shelling out money? Maybe she found me attractive. Is that so far fetched?" Tim was pushing all his buttons, and he knew it.

"Calm down. I'm just messing with you. Of course she found you attractive. Hell, I find you attractive." Tim's voice was a little too loud for the small restaurant, and several heads turned into their direction.

Daniel rolled his eyes, and Tim just chuckled. "Relax. This is San Francisco. Nobody cares."

"Easy for you to say, you're a Californian. I'm from New York, remember?"

"How could I forget? Maybe you should move out here. Life's much more relaxed. I bet even you wouldn't be that uptight here."

"I'm not uptight," Daniel barked indignantly. Maybe just a little uptight.

"Of course, you are. But I think the San Francisco air is having a good effect on you already. Barely in town for a few days, and here you are, dating an escort. Now if that's not liberating, I don't know what." Tim sipped from his wine.

"Would you stop calling her an escort. Her name is Sabrina."

"How are you going to introduce her to Mamma and Dad?" Tim liked referring to Daniel's parents as if they were his own.

Daniel's mouth dropped open.

"Don't look at me like you haven't thought this through. I know you too well."

"What the hell are you talking about?" Daniel gave him a frustrated stare.

"When did you last take a couple of days off to go out of town on a vacation?"

Daniel opened his mouth, but Tim stopped him.

"Don't answer that, 'cause I know the answer. You can't remember when. Funny. During the entire time you dated Audrey you didn't spend one lazy weekend with her anywhere. Yet suddenly, you're taking a weekend off to take the hot little Sabrina up into the wine country without a business meeting in sight. So why would that be? Go ahead, you can answer that."

Daniel shook his head. "I'd rather hear your theory."

"Very well. 'Cause the high and mighty *I-don't-want-any-messy-relationships* Daniel has finally fallen for a real woman. No more plastic girlfriends like Audrey et al. Congratulations, my friend, I hope she feels the same way."

Tim lifted his glass in toast to Daniel, who just sat there, shell-shocked. He'd known it deep down, but had been unwilling to accept it, because it seemed so impossible. The jealous rage he'd felt when he'd seen Hannigan and thought he'd been one of her *clients* had been a clear indication of his feelings for her, but he'd tried to ignore it.

He, Daniel Sinclair, didn't fall in love with a woman in two days, especially not one he, at the time, had believed to be a prostitute. Yet, the fact that he'd treated her more like a date than an escort from the very beginning, had shown him that there'd been something special right from the start. Right from the moment when she'd stood at the door to his hotel room.

"Tim, I think I need help." Daniel gave his friend a serious look. "I can't afford to screw this up. And I'm already walking on thin ice with her."

Tim rubbed his hands. "In that case, we'll have to devise a little plan of action." He looked at his watch. "We have about fourteen hours, plenty of time to put a few things together. Come on, eat up, we can't dilly dally."

Chapter Eight

When the door bell rang exactly at nine o'clock, Sabrina knew who it was. She took her small travel bag and cast a look back at Holly, who stood in the door to her bedroom wiping the sleep out of her eyes.

"Breathe." Holly gave her an encouraging smile. "You can do this."

Without another word, Sabrina left the flat to meet him downstairs. Daniel looked relaxed in his shorts and polo shirt as he leaned casually against the hood of a red convertible. A large grin spread over his face as soon as she approached him.

Sabrina felt his eyes taking her in from head to toe despite the fact that they were hidden behind his sunglasses. She'd opted for a pair of shorts and a tank top as well as flat sandals. The weather report had promised a scorching hot weekend even in San Francisco, which was unusual. Up in Sonoma County, where they were headed, it would be a good ten to fifteen degrees hotter.

He greeted her with a friendly kiss on the cheek. "You look great."

After stowing her luggage in the trunk, he held the door of the car open for her and closed it after she'd taken her seat.

Minutes later, they were weaving through light traffic making their way to Golden Gate Bridge. It turned out to be a smart idea to leave early. Since it would be a fog-free day, San Franciscans would use the opportunity to soak up the sunshine at the various beaches around the Bay and the Ocean, and all roads leading out of town would be choking with traffic later.

Daniel made light conversation during the entire drive north, telling her about his family back East, his temperamental Italian mother, and his American father.

"No, I'm an only child, unfortunately. I always hoped for a little brother or sister, but it just didn't happen. They sure were trying, constantly." He gave her a sheepish sideways glance.

Sabrina laughed. "Are you saying you listened in on your parents having sex? That's gross!"

"It was hard to avoid. My mother is a very vocal woman. When I couldn't take it any longer, I finally got them to move my room to the other side of the house. Now that was a relief. As much as I love my parents, I didn't need the mental picture of them in bed together. It can really screw a kid over."

"Have you inherited any of your mother's traits?" As soon as she asked the question, Sabrina realized how its meaning could be completely misconstrued. And it was. Nothing escaped him.

"You tell me."

Her cheeks burned, and she knew she blushed down to the roots of her hair. Of course he had to pick up on the sexual meaning, typical him.

"I mean her temperament and her physical appearance." Sabrina tried to bring their conversation back on the straight and narrow.

"I'm not exactly a five foot two, curvy woman," he started, grinning from one ear to the next, "but I did inherit her dark complexion, her eyes, and her hair. I got my physique from Dad. He's quite an athlete. He's a great tennis player, and he swims daily. Mamma tries to keep up with him as much as she can."

Sabrina looked at him from the side and could instinctively imagine what he would look like thirty years older. Still the same flawless body but with some gray around his temples, a few more lines on his face, around his mouth and eyes, and still the same wicked smile.

"It's nice to have parents, who are still together and love each other," she mused.

"Yours aren't? Still together, I mean?" Daniel asked somewhat surprised.

She shook her head. "They divorced when I was fourteen, but at least they both stayed in the same town. During the week, I lived with Mom and on the weekend with Dad."

"Were you torn between them?"

"Sometimes. But frankly, I learned to play them."

Daniel raised an eyebrow. "You mean manipulate them?" A smile curled around his lips.

"That sounds harsh. I just knew how to get the best of both worlds. Nothing wrong with that, especially since I was in the middle of it all."

"So, how good are you at that manipulation game of yours?"

Sabrina laughed. "As a businessman you should know never to show all your cards. It's like playing poker."

"The only poker I'm interested in playing with you is strip poker," he retorted quickly but kept his eyes on the road.

She had to hand it to him. No matter what subject they were talking about, he managed to bring it back to sex every time. He might have promised her to not force her to have sex with him, and she trusted him to keep his word, but it didn't mean he was going to keep the subject off the table.

She'd have to be careful not to have him trip her up. If she wasn't vigilant this weekend, he'd have her tumbling into his arms in no time. She couldn't allow herself to let her guard down and give him another chance at hurting her. The damage he'd caused was already big enough.

Even though she'd accepted his explanation about his ex-girlfriend Audrey, she wasn't truly convinced that he was honest with her. No man would spend thousands of dollars for a few days with an escort without expecting to have sex with her. He was up to something, and she was determined to get to the bottom of it.

After they left the highway to find the turnoff that would bring them to the little bed and breakfast he'd reserved for them, they go lost for a short time. She was surprised when Daniel stopped to ask a passing farmer for directions. She knew plenty of men who would have rather driven around in circles than admitted they were lost.

He smiled at her as if he knew what she was thinking. "We should be there in a couple of minutes."

The place he'd chosen was a dream. They'd arrived at a working vineyard, which operated a small bed and breakfast. But unlike other bed and breakfasts, this one had a few little cottages dotted around the large estate. One of those would be theirs.

Daniel dropped their bags in the living room as they stepped into the place after picking up the key from the main house. There was a small kitchen to the left of them. It would be sufficient to make coffee in the morning.

Sabrina walked through to the bedroom. It was furnished with a Queen size bed, night stands, and a dresser as well as a couple of comfortable chairs. The en-suite bathroom had both a tub and a shower. The French doors in the bedroom led out to a large terrace spanning the entire width of the cottage.

But the view was something else. As soon as Sabrina opened the doors and stepped out onto it, she was mesmerized. Looking down from the top of the hill on which the cottage was perched, the vineyard stretched out into the valley. Gently rising slopes on either side surrounded the rows and rows of vines.

"It's beautiful," she whispered.

"Breathtaking," she heard his voice behind her, his breath caressing her neck. "You think you'll enjoy staying here for the weekend? Even if you have to put up with me?"

She turned her head and gave him a soft smile. "Even if I have to put up with you."

His eyes caressed her, but he made no attempt to touch or kiss her, which surprised her. "Come, let's go for a walk around the vineyard."

Daniel offered his hand, and she took it without hesitation as they left the cottage and wandered down the path, which led through the vines. The sun was already hot and pleasantly touched her skin while she strolled along the dirt paths with him, her fingers intertwined with his.

It was a casual touch, not the purely sexual touch she was used to by him. She wondered what had brought this change about. Even when they'd met at the coffee shop the night before, he'd been full of barely contained desire. But now he'd turned into the sweet guy from next door. He was funny and entertaining, and apart from the few sexual innuendos he'd made in the car, he'd shown no sign of wanting to seduce her.

It had felt as if the further away from San Francisco they'd driven, the more he'd left his seductive side behind. His easy going demeanor relaxed her, and it felt as if the tension from the last few days finally left her body. Even the unpleasant and potentially dangerous situation with Hannigan faded into the distance.

Daniel helped her up a steep path, and they suddenly stood on a little grassy plateau. Several trees provided shade. The view was three hundred and sixty degrees and stunning. Rolling hills, trees, vines, a small stream in the distance. It looked as if taken right out of a tourist brochure.

As Sabrina examined the plateau closer, she noticed a large blanket with a basket resting underneath one of the trees. He followed her gaze.

"I hope you're hungry. I had a little picnic basket put together for us."

Daniel smiled when he saw her surprised face.

"Wow."

They spread out on the blanket, and he took out the food from the basket: bread, cheeses, olives, spreads, cold cuts, and of course a bottle of wine. No picnic in the wine country would be complete without wine.

Sabrina let herself be pampered. It had been very thoughtful of him to plan ahead and organize a lunch for them. She hadn't expected him to put this much thought and planning into the weekend.

Daniel poured the wine and handed her a glass.

"To a wonderful weekend," he toasted.

"To a wonderful weekend."

Before she had a chance to drink from her wine he bent to her and softly pressed his lips on hers. It only lasted a second before he pulled back and drank from his glass. Sabrina quickly took a sip to disguise the fact that the simple touch of his lips had completely ruffled her. When she'd felt him kissing her, she'd instantly wished for more, for a deeper connection and not the light, barely-there touch he'd teased her with.

"I'm glad you decided to join me."

"You didn't exactly leave me much of a choice." Sabrina took an olive and popped it into her mouth.

"Some people need a little persuasion." Daniel's smile was warm and kind. But she wasn't easily fooled. Underneath the sweet exterior the predator lurked. The man who'd practically devoured her in bed was still there. He hadn't just disappeared.

"Tell me, what's your plan?"

"My plan?" he gave her a sideways glance.

"For this weekend. It looks like you have a plan. This picnic didn't just appear out of nowhere. What other things do you have up your sleeve? Planning to soften me up, are you?"

"If I was, what makes you think I'd tell you what else you're in for? It would be showing my cards, wouldn't it?" He changed the subject. "Cheese?"

She took his offering, and they both started eating.

***

Daniel smiled inwardly. Sabrina was sharp, and there was little he'd get past her. She had to let him know that she was onto him, his cute pretend escort. Sure, he had a plan for the weekend, but there was no way he'd let her know the things he'd planned to sweep her off her feet and right into his arms.

With Tim's help, he'd come up with all kinds of ideas, and he would put as many as possible into practice. If by the end of the weekend she wasn't as taken with him as he was with her, he'd just have to try harder the next week. Failure was not an option.

Pouring the last of the wine into her glass, he noticed that she could hold her own. They were making light conversation during their meal, talking about wine, food, and vacations. Daniel lay back onto the blanket after he'd finished the last sip of wine. The lack of sleep was catching up with him.

Planning and preparing for the perfect weekend with Sabrina, even with Tim's help, had taken most of the night. He'd barely gotten two hours of sleep, and the wine had done the rest. His body couldn't hide the tiredness any longer.

In the morning, he'd left a message with his new lawyers about where they could reach him in case of absolute emergency but told them he didn't want to be disturbed. He'd even switched off his Blackberry, which he'd never done before.

"Do you mind if I close my eyes for a few minutes?" he asked her.

"Go ahead. It's nice up here. I might just nap a little too. The wine has made me a little tired."

Daniel saw her smile before he closed his eyes. Seconds later, he felt her shift on the blanket and knew she'd lain down next to him. He drifted off quickly, feeling a light breeze caress him. The tree provided sufficient shade for them to remain relatively cool despite the warmth of the sun.

He fell into a light dream, imagining her arms around him, her head resting on his chest and her even breathing soothing him. He could easily see himself with her, and not just in bed. He could see her by his side doing things couples did. But mostly, he could see her in his arms.

When he'd dated plastic women as Tim liked to call them, he'd never been very demonstrative with his feelings. Apart from lending a woman his arm to lead her to the table or to help her out of a car, he wasn't one to hold hands in public, let alone kiss. His girlfriends had always understood this.

With Sabrina, all he wanted to do was show the world that she was his. He wanted everybody to see that he was the one holding her hand, that he was the only one allowed to kiss her. When he'd left her with love bites after their first night together, he hadn't understood why he'd done it. He wasn't a teenager anymore, who did stupid things like that, and he'd certainly never done it to any of his previous girlfriends. But now that he knew the feelings he harbored for her, he knew that during their first night he'd instinctively branded her.

Daniel's chest felt heavy when he finally woke, and he felt something pressing against his thighs. As soon as he opened his eyes, he realized to his amazement what the cause of the weight was. His lips lifted into a smile.

Sabrina had snuggled into him and slept deeply, her head resting in the crook of his arm. Her arm lay heavy on his chest, and she'd placed one leg over his thighs. Just a look at her peaceful body sprawled over him, coupled with the feel of her bare legs touching the exposed skin on his shorts-clad thighs, was enough for his body to heat up.

Suddenly, the shade of the tree wasn't sufficient to cool him, nor was the light breeze getting even close to lowering his body temperature.

He was in deep shit. What had made him think he could spend the night in bed with her without touching her,? Even now, he could barely restrain himself from putting his hands on her to tug her even closer, or run his hand underneath her shorts to touch the soft skin of her ass. And now she was dressed. Tonight, she'd be naked or as close to naked as possible.

Panic gripped him. He'd never be able to go through with his plan. The coldest shower in the Antarctic wasn't sufficient to cool his thoughts or bring his erection under control once Sabrina was in his bed tonight.

How could he ever go through with his slow seduction to make her come to him when he would jump her bones the minute they were back at the cottage? Whose brilliant idea had that been? Oh yes, his own. Tim had doubted from the start that he'd ever be able to go through with it and had suggested he'd tell her the truth the minute they got out of town. One-nil for Tim.

***

Tim waved to catch Holly's attention when he saw her appear at the door to the coffee shop. She spotted him instantly and shuffled past the busy tables to plop down next to him on the couch. They kissed on the cheek.

"Darling, you have no idea what kind of night I've had," Tim complained theatrically.

"Don't get your knickers in twist, sweetie, at least you didn't have to deal with Sabrina crying her eyes out again." She let out a long breath of air.

"I love it when you talk dirty to me," he teased her.

"I wish, sweetie, I wish. For you I'd give up my job, honestly I would."

Tim gave her a friendly squeeze. "Sorry, darling, I can't change what I am. But if I could, I'd do it for you in a heartbeat."

She shrugged. "I think it's your turn to pay. I'll have a triple grande—"

He cut her off instantly. "Already ordered. I'm so way ahead of you." Her drink was called out by the barista and Tim got up to collect it for her.

Holly took a greedy gulp, then wiped the foam off her lips. "I needed that. I got up way too early to make sure Sabrina was really going to leave with him and not change her mind at the last minute."

"That's nothing. Danny kept me up half the night to organize everything for the weekend. Okay, so I volunteered to help him."

Holly raised an eyebrow.

"Fine. I convinced him that he needed to put some thought into this." Tim glanced at her and grinned. "I made him take a crash course in sensual massage."

"You did what?" Holly almost spilled her latte.

"I called my masseuse and had her teach him how to do a sensual massage. Trust me, Sabrina will thank us for it later. He's a fast learner. And he's motivated."

Holly shook her head. "Don't you think we're taking this too far?"

Tim made a dismissive hand movement. "After all you've told me about Sabrina over the years, I'm telling you they're perfect for each other."

"I'm having second thoughts. She's going to get hurt. We should have never done this. What the hell were we thinking?" There was concern in Holly's voice.

Sheepishly, Tim looked at her. "Did I mention that he's fallen in love with her?"

Holly's mouth dropped open. "Are you sure?"

He tossed her an offended look. "Do I know Danny, or don't I know Danny?"

"Did he tell you?"

"No, I told him. He needed a bit of a jolt. But he's on board now. I saw it in his eyes, the full shebang. Rattled him quite a bit, but he'll be fine." He smiled self-assuredly. "I'm sure everything will fall into place when he tells her the truth."

Holly shook her head. "And when do you think there'll ever be the right time for the truth to come out? Sabrina is so paranoid about getting hurt again that she'll just shut down."

"Don't worry, he'll handle it. Our work is done. And a great job we did. Don't you think so?"

"That's still not decided. By the way, great timing with the phone call. Sabrina bought it instantly. Didn't suspect anything. Who was the girl?"

"A waitress I know. It told her to pretend it's a monologue for an audition."

"I wish we could have orchestrated this differently though. Sabrina is going to be so mad at me when she finds out." Holly bit her lower lip.

"Hey, not my fault. I wanted to set them up on a blind date, but he didn't want a date. I couldn't just let that opportunity slip through my fingers. Who knows how long we would have had to wait for another one. It was perfect timing. Believe me, even though I never met that ex-girlfriend of his, I know the type. None of those women he went out with were right for him. I love him like a brother. I'm not having him end up with some money-grabbing plastic bitch. He needs a real woman with real feelings." His tone was adamant.

Holly nodded in agreement. "Well, here's his chance. She's got feelings all right. I just hope your friend can handle that. I hope he's not out to play her."

"Oh, he'll play, but he'll play for keeps. When he gets something into his head, he's not going to stop until he's got what he wants. And I tell you, he wants her. He wanted her already when he still thought she was an escort. Deep down he doesn't give a damn about conventions. Even if she was an escort, he'd still want her. Even if it meant he'd have to tell his parents that he's in love with a prostitute, even though for Mamma's sake I'm sure he's glad she's not. Not that he'd ever tell her."Tim chuckled softly, and she jabbed him in the ribs. "There's nothing wrong with being an escort, and would you please not call it prostitute," she snorted.

He hugged her. "Absolutely right. It's all a matter of price."

"You're such an ass sometimes," she retorted laughingly.

"I suspect that's why you love me?" Tim smirked.

"Why did you never try to set me up with him?"

He gave her an incredulous look. "What? And lose my best female friend? What am I, completely selfless? Don't you know me at all? And besides, you're not his type."

She sighed. "He said as much when I met him. God, he's even hotter in person than on the pictures you showed me."

"Don't I know it? And don't worry, I'll find you somebody else. But not yet. I'm not quite ready to let go. Who else can I call at two in the morning when I'm feeling blue?"

Holly shook her head and laughed. "Selfish bastard."

Chapter Nine

Daniel needed a cold shower, and he needed it now. They'd returned to the cottage, and just looking at Sabrina's legs sticking out from her shorts as he followed her inside made him feel like walking on a bed of hot coals. Barefoot.

"Will you excuse me for a few minutes please?" he managed to press out before he made a mad dash for the bathroom. Locking the door behind him, he stripped and jumped into the shower. She was probably thinking he was crazy, but it was either that or him wrestling her to the ground, tearing her clothes off.

When she'd finally awoken in his arms, she'd looked embarrassed, and he'd let it go and not made any sexual comments about it. But it didn't mean he could forget about how her body had felt. It had reminded him of all the things they'd done in and out of bed the first two evenings they'd spent together.

The cold water ran down his hot body but did nothing to ease his throbbing erection. Like a soldier on the parade grounds, it just stood there, straight, hard, and unyielding. Who had ever created the rumor that a cold shower got rid of an erection? It obviously was some old wives tale.

For sure it wasn't working for him. Damn! He couldn't go out there and face her with that thing. It was like a loaded gun, liable to go off at any second. No safety on. There was only one other surefire way to unload that weapon.

As Daniel took his cock into his hand, he closed his eyes and imagined Sabrina in the shower with him. Her hand touching him. Her mouth. Her tongue. Her hand tightening around his shaft, sliding up and down on it, first slow and then faster, harder. Until he was panting.

It didn't take much for him to find release. Within seconds, he came and shot his seed against the tile wall of the shower. Daniel only hoped that this release would help him get through the rest of the day and the night. But he had his doubts.

He started to understand the depth of his feelings, and his body yearned for a joining with her. He had to get himself under control. After what Holly had told him about Sabrina, he knew she had to be wooed gently. Ramming her with his rod wasn't the way to go. Not yet anyway.

When he stepped back into the bedroom, again fully dressed, he looked around for her. He found Sabrina on the terrace, where she'd already spotted the next surprise he'd planned for her.

The staff of the inn had organized a professional massage table and set it up outside. She looked at him, her green eyes questioning him.

"What is this?"

He was sure she'd seen a massage table before, but that wasn't her question. "It's exactly what it looks like. Are you ready for your massage?"

"When's the masseuse coming?"

He could tell she liked the idea of a massage and smiled. "He's already here." Sabrina looked at him, and within seconds realization washed over her face.

"You?"

Daniel nodded. "I took a class."

More like a crash course. Last night. He handed her the bathrobe which lay on the massage table.

"Get undressed and put this on."

He nodded toward the bathroom.

"You can't be serious." It was only half a protest.

"I've seen you naked before. There's no need to be shy. I promise you, you'll enjoy it."

***

Sabrina contemplated whether to allow him to massage her. The idea of a relaxing massage pleased her, but she was unsure as to her reaction to feeling his hands on her naked skin. It was one hell of a temptation, and she wondered if it would be safe. He'd been a gentleman all day up till now.

Even when she'd found herself waking up with her body half covering his, he'd not used the situation to his own advantage. She knew that she'd been the one who'd cuddled up to him and not the other way around. Just before she'd fallen asleep, she'd felt the urge to be close to him, and her mind had already shut off. Her instincts had taken over, and she'd scooted over to him. Her body had just done what it wanted and molded itself to his.

He'd placed a gentle kiss on the top of her head before she'd freed herself from his body but had made no other attempt at touching her. Well, their agreement had been that he was allowed to kiss her, but she'd thought he'd meant those steamy, hot, smoldering kisses he'd bestowed on her during their first two evenings of passion. Not the chaste pecks he'd given her today.

"I'll be right back," Sabrina announced, took the bathrobe and went back inside. Less than two minutes later she was back, wearing the bathrobe with not a stitch of clothing underneath it.

It was time to see whether his kisses would remain this chaste after he'd massaged her. She stopped her own thoughts. Why the hell was she even thinking that? She should be happy that he kept his tongue to himself. His tongue. The thought of it caressing her skin …

No! She shouldn't think of it. He'd basically blackmailed her into this weekend and this booking, and she'd be out of her mind if she let herself be lulled into this again. She had to think of herself and the fact that in a few days he'd be gone, and she'd be miserable, because she'd fallen for a man who only saw her as a toy to play with.

Sabrina dropped her bathrobe and lay down on her stomach. She was fully aware of his gaze on her and how he swallowed hard when she stood before him entirely nude for a mere few seconds.

Daniel placed a large soft towel over the length of her body.

"I hope you like the scent of lavender." His voice sounded raspy.

"Mmm hmm," she replied and relaxed into the comfortable massage table.

She felt his hands graze her shoulders as he pulled the towel down to her hips. The sound of his hands lathering themselves with oil followed, and she went rigid in anticipation of his touch.

The instant she felt his strong hands on her back, starting with long strokes from her shoulders down to her waist, she realized that she would have a snowball's chance in hell of resisting him if he tried to seduce her. But it was too late to withdraw now. She was in his hands, in his very capable hands.

An involuntary moan escaped her as Daniel's hands continued to rhythmically glide up and down her back. She clenched her jaw together to avoid any more audible signs of pleasure. That was all she needed, letting him know that she was putty in his hands.

"Relax, baby," he whispered. "You're so tense."

Did he know everything that was going on inside her? "Why are you doing this?"

"You mean the massage?" he asked softly.

The sound of his voice alone made her want to melt. Combined with the gentle kneading motions of his hands, it proved to be a toxic cocktail for her already tortured heart.

"Everything, this weekend, the massage."

Daniel paused before he replied as if he didn't have an answer. "I like you, Holly."

She had to stop him from saying things like that. It couldn't lead to anything. It would just make things harder when they parted ways.

"Daniel, I'm an escort. You seem to keep forgetting that," she lied, hoping he could be brought back to the reality of their situation. Even though she wasn't an escort, he'd hired her as one, so for all intents and purposes she was his escort.

Sabrina heard him suck in his breath, and seconds ticked away in silence as he ran his hands down her spine, his thumbs putting just enough pressure on it to make her shiver with pleasure.

"I don't care what you are." His voice was unusually tense as if he was angry. "I can see what's underneath," he added, his voice a little softer than before.

Daniel was saying all the right things. If she'd met him under other circumstances, he'd be the perfect man. Kind and considerate, passionate and experienced, hot-blooded and strong. But the circumstances hadn't been right. He'd hired an escort because he'd just broken up with his girlfriend. He was on the rebound, and it was obvious that he didn't want to have another relationship. Why else hire an escort? It guaranteed sex without the strings attached.

Sabrina didn't comment but instead concentrated on his hands. Every time his hands stroked down to her waist, his fingertips reached lower, gently caressing the top of her ass. And every time, she wished he'd go lower.

As if Daniel could tell what she wanted, his hands finally left her back altogether and slid underneath the towel to stroke her round cheeks. Instantly, another guttural moan escaped her lips. His movements turned into a caress and had nothing to do with the massaging strokes he'd lavished on her back and shoulders.

His fingers blazed trails of fire over her cheeks, then rode down to her thighs before reversing and travelling back up again.

Sabrina felt heat shoot through her belly, and within seconds moisture pooled at the juncture of her thighs. The way this man could arouse her should be illegal. She had to stop herself from allowing her body to arch toward his hands.

If he continued a few minutes longer, she knew she'd come without him ever touching her any more intimately. Her body trembled lightly at the thought of it, and she tensed trying to control herself as not to scream and ask him to take her.

"I'm sorry," Daniel suddenly said and pulled his hands away from her.

Disappointment swept through her. He covered her back and shoulders with the towel before pulling it back from one of her legs. The soft late afternoon breeze cooled her hot leg but not for long.

After pouring more oil on his hands, Daniel placed them on her leg and slowly moved down from the top of her thigh to the tip of her toes. Did he really think those strokes would keep her from getting aroused again? He surely had to have noticed what he'd done by caressing her ass.

With every stroke, her skin turned hotter. As he ran his hands from the back of her knee up her thigh again, she held her breath. Would the hand which ran along the inside of her thigh reach high enough to notice how wet she was? Would he let his finger slide high enough to feel her moist flesh or even penetrate her?

To her dismay, Daniel stopped before he even got close and then reversed his stroke and moved back down. His hands felt like sizzling irons on her skin, just hotter and softer. She knew she kept a lot of tension in her body, but she felt how he worked through the knots in her muscles.

Sabrina just wanted to let go and not think of anything, and the more she concentrated on his hands and forgot about everything else, the more she felt her muscles relax.

She'd deal with everything else later. For now, she only wanted to bathe in the warmth of his hands and the tenderness of his strokes. She didn't want to read anything else into it.

"You have wonderful hands."

She could hear the smile in his words when he answered. "You have a beautiful body."

"Do you often give massages?" She envied his girlfriends, and a knot formed in her stomach at the thought of him lavishing another woman with this kind of attention.

"This is my first."

She was startled. "Your first? That's impossible. You're amazing." She didn't believe him. Nobody was this talented.

"It's easy with a pliable body like yours."

Daniel pulled the towel back over her legs, covering her completely.

"How are you feeling?"

Disappointed that it was over, she wanted to say, but didn't. "Weak."

He chuckled. "I think it's called relaxed, not weak."

Sabrina turned her head to look at his face. His lips wore a soft smile, but his eyes couldn't hide his desire for her. For several seconds, she didn't say anything and only looked at him.

"Thank you. It was wonderful."

"You're welcome." He looked almost tortured before he turned away from her gaze. "Just keep resting here as long as you want to."

And with those words he went back inside. A minute later, she heard the shower. She knotted her eyebrows. He'd taken a shower only an hour earlier. Even though it had been pretty warm out, it wasn't exactly scorching hot in the late afternoon sun, and besides, the terrace was shady.

Sabrina turned her head out toward the valley and the vineyards. It was a beautiful sight, and life could be perfect if only circumstances were different. She sighed.

***

His second cold shower of the day didn't do any more good than the first. He was an idiot. He should have never let the real Holly talk him into continuing this charade. He should have gone with his gut instinct and told Sabrina the truth as soon as he'd walked out of the Escort Service's offices.

Now he was stuck between a rock and an even rockier place. On the one hand, he wanted nothing more than to make love to her, but on the other, he'd promised her she'd be the one to initiate sex. If he came up with any more brilliant ideas like this one, he'd be the next addition to the Darwin Awards for eliminating himself from the gene pool.

What made him think Sabrina would come to him if only he wouldn't hit on her for a day? The massage had left him completely and utterly hot and bothered, and *he* was the one who'd given it, for God's sake. Sure, she'd enjoyed it, but other than that, he'd seen no reaction from her that would have told him she wanted to be touched in a more sexual way.

When he'd caressed her delectable ass, she'd tensed under his hands, and he'd had to pull away in order not to destroy the moment altogether. She'd kept her wall up the entire time. Her comment that she was an escort had basically insinuated that she didn't want any other relationship with him. She'd put him in his place.

That thought was what finally brought his erection down, not the cold water of the shower. She didn't want him. As Holly had said to him, Sabrina hadn't had sex in three years, and she hadn't been in a relationship. What if she'd enjoyed sex with him only because she hadn't had any in such a long time, but in the end she really didn't want anything else?

Daniel felt depressed when he stepped out of the shower and dried off. Putting a towel around his lower body, he went into the bedroom. Still consumed with his thoughts about her, he dropped the towel, reached for a new set of clothes and slowly got dressed.

When he turned, he saw Sabrina standing in the door, which connected to the living room. Her cheeks were rosy. How long had she been standing there? It didn't matter. He wasn't shy, and she'd seen him naked before. But her pink cheeks suggested that he'd embarrassed her.

"I should take a shower too," she announced and brushed past him on her way to the bathroom, averting her eyes.

"I've made dinner reservations for seven o'clock. Take your time."

Daniel looked at his watch. He could do with a drink, but he knew he'd be driving them to the restaurant, and he wanted some wine with his dinner. No drink, then, for now.

He plopped down on the couch in the living room and switched on the TV. Anything to distract himself from the thought that she stood in the shower, naked, the water pearling off her perfect skin. Did this cottage have air conditioning? His eyes scanned the room. No air conditioning.

Why was he so hot? Had he gotten too much sun earlier in the day? He shook his head. No, it was more a case of having gotten too much of Sabrina under his skin. It appeared it was pretty much an incurable condition by now.

Daniel watched the early evening news but barely listened to the anchor. From the corner of his eye, he saw a movement and looked to the side. Sabrina had finished her shower already, and through the open door to the bedroom he saw that she'd come out of the bathroom only dressed in a towel.

Damn, didn't she know that the bedroom door was open? Seconds later, he panted heavily when as he saw her drop the towel and pick through her bag for some new clothes. Hell, didn't she realize that he could see her from where he was? She was killing him. She literally would be the death of him.

Instead of being a gentlemen and looking the other way, he let his eyes glide over her naked body and watched her get dressed. First, she pulled up the tiny black panties, then she stepped into yet another thin summer dress, similar to the one she'd worn the night they'd gone to the cooking class. His hand instinctively went to his crotch, where he felt the familiar bulge that had become his constant companion since he'd met her.

Fuck, could this woman not wear a bra? Did she have to slip into the dress without it, knowing that with every step she'd make tonight, her gorgeous boobs would bounce suggestively?

As she bent down to put on her high heeled sandals, he admired her shapely legs and hallucinated about how he'd throw her over the dresser, rip her panties off and plunge himself into her.

Daniel jumped up from the couch and headed to the kitchen, ripped the freezer open and stuck his head into it. The cool air hurt, but he needed it. Slowly, his breathing returned to normal.

"What are you doing?" Sabrina's voice startled him, and he hit his head on the freezer door as he pulled out.

"Ouch!" Great, how would he explain this? "Nothing. Just checking if we have ice cubes."

She raised an eyebrow but didn't comment any further. She looked stunning. Her skin glowed both from the sun she'd gotten in the afternoon and the oil he'd used on her during the massage. The scent of lavender was still all around her.

She wore practically no make-up. Not that she needed it. Her face was flawless, and her eyelashes so naturally think that no mascara would have added anything to her expressive eyes.

"I didn't expect you to be done so quickly." Daniel definitely hadn't. None of his girlfriends had ever gotten showered and dressed in under an hour, let alone in under fifteen minutes.

Sabrina shrugged. "Sorry to disappoint you."

"Come, we might as well drive into town early and do a little sightseeing before dinner." Anything to get out of this cottage and the temptation to strip her naked.

The little town of Healdsburg was centrally located in between Alexander Valley, Chalk Hill and Dry Creek Valley. Daniel wasn't disappointed in the restaurant Tim had recommended, and judging by Sabrina's appetite, she loved the food too. When he'd massaged her, he'd noticed that her curves were fuller than those of any of his ex-girlfriends, who'd barely ever eaten more than a little salad or some sashimi for fear of gaining a pound or two.

He liked to feel the roundness of her hips and the fullness of her breasts, and it reminded him that he hadn't touched her breasts in far too long. Severe withdrawal symptoms made themselves known in the form of uncomfortable pangs in his abdomen.

During dinner, their conversation centered around observations about the wine country. He avoided anything that could be construed in a sexual way, and Sabrina seemed to do the same. On the drive back to the cottage, they were both quiet. He knew what was on her mind, because it was also on his mind: they'd be sharing a bed tonight.

Chapter Ten

Sabrina had felt the tension all evening. There'd been an awkward silence between them on the way back in the car. As soon as they'd gotten to the cottage, Daniel had switched on the TV and installed himself on the couch.

She took her time in the bathroom, but at some point she couldn't stall any longer and, dressed in a simple short cotton nightdress, she went into the bedroom. It was still empty. She slipped under the covers and wondered when he'd finally come to bed.

She'd missed his touch and his kisses more than she wanted to admit. There really was no way around it. She wanted him, and she didn't want to deny herself anymore. To hell with the consequences. By now Holly had probably stocked up their freezer with enough ice cream to see her through the worst once Daniel was gone.

The sound of the TV ceased, and a few seconds later Daniel came into the bedroom and closed the door behind him. He went straight for the bathroom. Sabrina shook her head when she heard the shower again. This would have to stop. And she would make sure it did.

Daniel couldn't have looked any more tortured if he'd just had his teeth pulled. And she knew that she was the reason for it. She wasn't being fair to him. He'd paid to spend time with her and to enjoy himself, and she was spoiling his fun. And her own fun at the same time.

The bathroom door opened, and he stepped out, dressed only in his boxer shorts. With every step he made toward the bed, her heart beat faster. She hoped to find the courage to do what she needed to do.

The mattress moved when he lowered himself onto the bed and slid under the covers. He reached for the light on the nightstand and switched it off.

"Good night, Holly."

He made no attempt to move closer to her or to even kiss her goodnight. Her heart beat up into her throat now, but she couldn't go back.

"How are those cold showers working for you?"

She felt him jolt up, and seconds later the light came back on. He sat upright in bed and turned to her. His face looked angry. This evidently hadn't been the right approach.

"I think it's better I sleep on the couch."

Before he could get out off bed, Sabrina put her hand on his arm and pulled him back. "No."

He gave her a startled look but didn't say anything.

"You promised we'd be sharing a bed, and you also promised you'd kiss me. Are you planning on backing out on both those promises?"

He raised his eyebrows but still didn't talk.

"Damn it, Daniel, you haven't kissed me all day, and you're moping around like somebody stole your lollipop. Why the hell don't you take what you want? You sure paid for it." Now she felt anger boiling up in her. How could a man be so stubborn?

He finally seemed to find his voice again. "I don't take what's not offered freely," he hissed.

"What do you want me to do? Wear a sign saying *fuck me*? I can't do that."

"I won't sink so low as to force a woman to have sex with me when she obviously doesn't want me, no matter whether I paid for it or not. You made it pretty clear today that you don't want me. I should have never talked you into this weekend."

"What?" She thought she'd given him sufficient signals that she wanted him to touch her. Had he completely forgotten the massage and how she'd shivered under his touch?

"Don't play with me. Every time I touch you, you tense up."

Oh God, he'd completely misread her. She'd have to be much more obvious to get the message to him. Drawing on all her courage, she slid closer to him.

"Daniel, please." Sabrina looked into his eyes, but he didn't seem to understand. She took his hand and slowly moved it, placing it on her breast. "Make love to me."

"Because I paid for it?"

She shook her head. "Because I want you to. Because I need to feel you inside of me."

His other hand went to her face, cupping it gently. Daniel searched her eyes as if to determine whether she meant what she'd said. "Are you sure?"

She could feel his breath on her face. "Kiss me and you'll find out."

The instant she felt his lips on hers, her heart leapt, and she felt as if she'd faint. But his lips kept her conscious. There was no denying their chemistry. His kiss released all the pent up tension from the day. Without hesitation, she responded to him, demanded he play with her tongue and invade her mouth.

She clung to him with a desperation she'd never known, until she suddenly felt him pull away. Stunned, she looked at him. Had she put him off with her behavior?

"We have to talk," he said in a serious voice.

"No. No talking. I want to feel you."

He grabbed her wrists before she could pull him back against her body. "Baby, I need you to understand something."

No. She didn't want to know anything. She didn't want to face reality, not the reality they were in anyway.

"Look at me." His tone was insistent. "If we do this tonight, if we make love, you're mine. There will be no backing down. I won't take no for an answer after this. Do you understand?"

Sabrina nodded. She understood. As long as he was in San Francisco and for the entire time he'd booked her, he'd demand that she have sex with him, and he wouldn't accept any more excuses. Yes, she understood. And she would comply, because she wanted him.

"Yes."

"God, I missed you," Daniel exclaimed and swept her back into his arms. He chuckled softly. "I have to warn you, those cold showers didn't do anything to cool my desire for you."

Sabrina laughed. "I don't know why you bothered. You almost made me come on the massage table. You could have had me right there and then."

Daniel gave her a surprised look. "But you tensed up."

"Because I was about sixty seconds away from an orgasm."

He kissed her softly. "I'm such an idiot. How can I make it up to you?"

"I can think of a thing or two ... or three ... or four." She smirked.

***

Daniel laughed out loud and hugged her tightly, his laughter rippling through his body. Suddenly everything was perfect again. Sabrina had come to him and admitted she wanted him. And he'd told her that he wanted her for good, and she'd accepted it. They'd work out the details of their lives together later. But now, all he wanted was to make love to her. He'd already waited far too long.

Though he could feel her breasts through her thin nightgown, he decided she wore far too many clothes. He'd make it a rule that from now on she wouldn't be allowed to wear anything in bed. Ever.

His mouth was greedy when he captured hers, because he was hungrier for her than he'd ever been. The knowledge that he loved the woman in his arms made every touch and kiss double as sweet. He hadn't declared his love yet, but he knew she could feel it. Soon he'd make it official.

But for tonight, he would just savor her first step, savor that she'd come to him. He knew she needed more time for all implications to sink in, but she'd already made a large leap forward by acknowledging that she was his.

The only small hurdle he still had to jump over was to let her know that he was aware she wasn't an escort. But this wasn't a talk for tonight. After twenty-four hours of lovemaking she'd be ready to have that conversation, because by then she would have realized just how much he loved her. He'd make sure of that.

As Daniel freed her from her nightgown and slipped out of his boxers, he was finally able to feel Sabrina the way he'd wanted to all day. Naked skin on naked skin, lips locked, legs intertwined. Possessively, his hand moved to the soft curves of her ass and tugged her closer into him. With a sigh, she surrendered.

"Baby, I've never been happier," he murmured into her ear as he proceeded to kiss the tempting curve of her graceful neck down to the dip on the base of it.

Her hands roamed over his chest exploring him, but before he could even register her touch, she moved south. A second later, she wrapped her hand around his erection. A deep moan originating in his gut traveled up to be released from his lips.

With one touch, this woman could completely undo him. His woman, he corrected himself. The power she had over him was frightening yet exciting at the same time.

"Stop, baby, please. Or you're going to make me come instantly."

As he looked into her face, he saw a naughty smile spread over her lips. "A little sensitive, are we?"

"Says the woman who almost came on the massage table," he joked. "Which reminds me. What exactly was it that set you off?"

Before she could protest, he flipped her onto her stomach. "I think I should find out in order to know for the future."

"I don't think I should give away secrets like that," Sabrina teased him.

He kneeled next to her and put his hands onto her back. "I'll just have to figure it out for myself then." And his hands went to work, slowly moving along her neck and shoulders, before diving deeper, stroking along her spine and reaching the curve of her lower back.

Daniel noticed a change in her breathing and knew exactly what direction to go. He shifted on the bed and, pushing his knee in between her thighs, he forced her to spread them wider to make space for him. She complied with an appreciative moan.

His erection grew harder and bigger as he looked at the enticing position he'd taken, nestling between her thighs with his hands on her hips. It was exactly the kind of position he wanted her in.

Softly, his hands massaged her cheeks, making circles on her skin, moving outwards to her hips and then back inwards and down to the apex of her thighs. Sabrina lifted her ass up toward his hands asking for more, and he saw the glistening entrance to her female core. Moisture oozed from her plump pink pussy.

Daniel slipped his hand down and touched the moist and warm flesh. Instantly, he was rewarded with her moan.

"I can guess what you want."

Sliding his fingers along the outside of her female folds, he sank his head onto her ass, planting kisses on her skin. Soon, his tongue came out to aid and licked every inch of her twin peaks. Her breathing told him that she was well on her way to a very satisfying conclusion. His teeth tugged at her skin, biting gently into her soft flesh.

Daniel felt her press against his hand, and he gave into her and slid his finger into her tight channel.

"Oh, Daniel!" Her voice was raspy and uncontrolled.

Continuing to bite and lick her ass, he added another finger and moved in and out of her moist core. Her body flexed under this touch, forcing him to move faster and harder.

"Please," she begged. "Fill me, now."

He was more than ready to join her. But where were those damn condoms? "Wait, condom."

"Nightstand, drawer, my side," Sabrina pushed out between pants.

Lifting himself up, but without pulling his fingers out of her, he struggled to reach the drawer, until he finally opened it and pulled a condom out. With his teeth he opened the wrapper.

"Sorry, baby." He needed both his hands to sheath himself. It took only seconds until he was ready and pulled her hips up to him.

"Now, Daniel, please."

His erection nudged at her center and sliced into her with one smooth, continuous, slow motion as he savored every inch he submerged into her. He pulled back and plunged in again, but it had been too much for her already. Her muscles clenched around him as her orgasm ripped through her, making him unable to hold on to his own control. He joined her in release as his cock jerked uncontrollably inside her.

Daniel felt a high he'd never felt before, as if he'd taken some drug and was floating. This was more than just sexual gratification. To be physically joined with the woman he loved, and to know the kind of heights they could drive each other to, brought with it the awareness that he'd found what he'd been unknowingly looking for all his life. His other half, the person who completed him.

As they collapsed, he rolled them to the side, spooning her. He showered Sabrina's neck with kisses, unable to stop showing his affection for her. With his hand, he smoothed her hair out of her face to look at her. She turned her face to him.

Her green eyes seemed darker than before, and she wore the look of a woman who seemed completely and utterly satisfied. Which wouldn't stop him from making love to her again very shortly. This night they wouldn't get any sleep, not if he could help it.

"Beats cold showers, hmm?" she asked.

Daniel laughed softly. "Beats everything else I've ever done in my life." Before Sabrina had a chance to react to his comment, he seared her lips with a passionate kiss.

***

No other man had ever been able to satisfy her the way he had. She knew she was kidding herself if she pretended she could just walk away from him after this week and go on with her life.

Sabrina looked into his brown eyes when he released her from his kiss and saw an ocean of tenderness in them. She knew Daniel was a passionate man, and maybe that's how he conducted all his affairs, giving a hundred percent of himself. But it didn't mean that after this week there'd be anything else.

She remembered how coldly he'd looked at his ex-girlfriend and knew she didn't want to be at the receiving end of that particular stare. Once he was through with somebody, his passion would turn to ice, and there was nothing she hated more than the cold. She would have to get out of this before he ever had a chance to turn on the ice machine.

For now of course, nothing of the coming ice storm was visible. On the contrary, he was hotter than ever. Already his hands roamed over her body again, and his lips and tongue followed, leaving a trail of fire on her skin.

She had to soak up what she could get, take what he was willing to give her. The need within her grew to monumental proportions, and it frightened her to know that he could awaken such primal emotions in her. But she wasn't frightened to ask for it anymore. In a week, it would be over, but for now she'd demand that he'd make love to her over and over again.

"I want you inside of me."

Was it a glimmer of pride she saw in his eyes? It didn't matter what it was, but only that Daniel responded to her the way she wanted him to.

"There's no place I'd rather be than inside of you."

This time when he entered her, their lovemaking was slow and deliberate. He was as hard and as thick as he'd been before, but now she could sense more of him as he slowly inched deeper into her and then just as slowly pulled out, only to repeat his movement a second later. And not for a single moment did he break eye contact with her as if he needed to read in her eyes what she felt while he impaled her again and again.

Small hitches of breath pushed out of her body at every stroke of his shaft inside her. Her body felt like it was on fire, a fire that was spreading from low in her belly outwards into all cells of her body.

Daniel whispered words in Italian to her, and even though she spoke no Italian, his tone told her that they were terms of endearment, a thought that warmed her even more. Knowing that he used the language his mother had taught him and which he associated with family and love, made her feel closer to him.

There was nothing else to do but to surrender to his touch, to let him sweep her up and carry her to heights she'd not been to before, to feel her body float as if it were as light as a cloud. To feel the waves crash into her as if she stood in the wake of a storm, to feel them rise to hurricane strength and yet to feel no fear, only anticipation as it reached its peak and then sweep through her body with more energy than an atom bomb.

Sabrina felt him explode with her, could see in his eyes the second he reached his climax, which seemed as powerful as hers. It was more than she could take. She felt the wetness in her eyes before she understood what was happening.

Only when she felt his lips kiss her eyes did she know he was kissing away her tears. Never had she felt so vulnerable and at the same time so safe. If she could hold on to this one moment and take it with her once he was gone, she knew she would be okay despite everything.

Later, she curled up beside him and felt his strong arms cradle her as if he never wanted to let her go.

"It's a shame we have to go back to San Francisco tomorrow," she lamented.

Daniel put his hand under her chin and pulled her face up to look at her. "Would you like us to stay longer?"

"I would love to, but I know you'll have to be back in the city for business."

"I can do everything I need to do from here. I'll tell the innkeeper tomorrow morning that we'll extend our stay."

Sabrina kissed him hard. She knew she'd have to call in sick, but she didn't care. Everybody was busy with the big new client anyway, and nobody took any notice of her, except for the person she didn't want to be noticed by: Hannigan. A few days away from the office was just what she needed. And she wanted to spend as much time with Daniel as she could.

"Thank you. I love it here."

He beamed. "I love it here too," he said and suggestively let his finger slide through her triangle of curls and dip into her moist core.

"Do you ever think of anything else?" she teased him.

"Sure. I also think of this." Daniel took her breast into his hand and kneaded it. "Or of this." He lowered his head to take her nipple into his mouth, sucking gently.

She had to laugh, and he joined in. He could be as playful as he was sensual and as passionate as he was tender.

Already she felt his cock rise from its short rest and found herself in need of a taste. She freed herself from his embrace.

"Where are you going?" He sounded disappointed as if even the shortest of separations was painful.

"Nowhere." She reversed her position on the bed so her head was on the same height as his growing erection.

"Mmm," he murmured appreciatively and pulled her thighs toward him so his face was right in between them, his mouth hovering at the entrance to her body.

With his erection coming to full height, her tongue flicked out and licked his shaft before working its way down to his balls. At the same time, she felt him dip his tongue into her. If she wanted to make him come before he turned her mind and body to mush with the things he did with his tongue, she would have to use all her skill.

As Sabrina fondled his balls and felt the soft sac tighten, she placed her lips around the head of his cock and slowly slid down, taking him inside her as deep as she could. For an instant, she felt him pause. Good, he was paying attention.

She loved his taste, just like the first night she'd tasted him. This time, she wanted more though. The first night, Daniel had stopped her, but he wouldn't get a chance this time. Her mouth was firmly locked onto his cock where it would stay until she was done with him.

She felt his tongue playing with her clit and had to stop her own actions for a brief moment to collect her strength. But then she continued with vigor. She took him deeper, sucked him harder and used her tongue to moisten his velvet skin. When she felt his breathing become choppy, she added her hand to the mix, first playing with his balls and then wrapping her fingers around his erection as she moved up and down it with her mouth.

She knew Daniel was close when she felt him lick her more frantically. He almost threw her off her course when he inserted a finger into her while continuing to suck her clit. But she wouldn't be deterred. Again she sucked him harder, squeezed her hand around him tighter until she finally felt a pulsating movement within him.

Yes, he was coming and while she felt him wanting to pull out, she held him firmly as he shot his warm seed into her mouth. She took it all in, not wanting to spill one drop.

"Oh, God."

Sabrina ignored his words as she milked him until she'd taken every drop of his life-giving fluids and swallowed. And still she didn't let go of him. Instead, she licked him clean with her tongue, until she suddenly felt him lick her clit with renewed intensity. Whether it was that or the fact that she'd sucked him and swallowed his seed, within seconds she was swept over the edge and erupted in a climax that rivaled his in intensity and duration.

Exhausted, they fell onto their backs.

It took minutes before she had the strength to turn on the bed and let herself be pulled back into his arms. Only when she felt his warm skin against hers, did her breathing slow down.

When Daniel looked at her, she knew he wanted to say something, but instead he just kissed her. No words were needed.

Chapter Eleven

Daniel woke with Sabrina firmly tucked in his arms. After a long night of lovemaking they'd finally fallen asleep around four in the morning. He'd never been one to linger in bed and even less to stay with a woman the morning after. It was different with her.

Not only had he slept better in her arms than he'd ever slept on his own, but even fully sated after their passionate night, he could now feel himself awaken to the same desire he'd had the night before. He was tempted to wake her, but instead contended himself with gazing into her peaceful face. Her chest rose with every breath she took, and he was fascinated just watching her.

Remembering everything they'd done the night before, he realized she needed some rest and some nourishment. He glanced at the clock. It was past ten o'clock, and she'd awoke with a rumbling stomach. They hadn't only burned up the sheets last night, they'd also burned calories—lots of them. And if he wanted her enticing curves to stay the way they were, he'd definitely have to feed her and replenish those calories. And he absolutely wanted those curves to remain just as they were. He couldn't imagine anything better under his hands.

He'd been at the verge of professing his love to her last night, but at the last minute had stopped himself. Not because he was unsure—he wasn't—but because he wanted everything else to be cleared between them first. Thinking back on what Holly had told him, he still wondered how to approach the subject. He didn't want to make a mistake.

Well, he certainly couldn't think on an empty stomach. As gently as he could, Daniel peeled himself out of her arms and got up. He took a quick shower before he jumped into the car to find the closest shop to pick up some morning pastries and decent coffee.

After stopping by at the main house to extend their stay indefinitely, he came back and found the bedroom empty. He'd wanted to surprise Sabrina with breakfast in bed, but she'd already woken up. He heard the shower and was pleased to find that the door to the bathroom was unlocked.

It wasn't an opportunity he could pass up. Quickly, he stripped naked and snuck into the bathroom. She stood in the shower in her glorious nakedness and hadn't seen or heard him come in. He let his eyes gaze over her luscious body and took in a deep breath. He'd never get enough of her.

Silently, he approached the shower and stepped in behind Sabrina. He gathered her in his arms and knew he'd surprised her when she let out a startled shriek.

"Good morning," he whispered into her ear while at the same time nibbling on her earlobe.

"You came back," she said as she turned in his arms and looked up at him.

"Nothing can keep me from you for long. But I did have to get us some breakfast. Hungry?"

She nodded, and he saw a flicker of desire in her eyes. "Mmm hmm."

He didn't need more than that as an invitation. "How hungry?"

"Just as hungry as you." Her gaze went lower and rested on his growing erection, which was already pressing against her stomach. Sabrina could set him ablaze with just a glance. His hunger for food was instantly forgotten.

As soon as her arms went around his neck, he kissed her. It had been too many hours since he'd last felt her lips on his and danced with her tongue. Within seconds, he was fully aroused and to his dismay realized he'd left the damn condoms in the bedroom.

He'd never had sex with a woman without condoms, not because of fear of disease, but mainly because he'd never trusted any of his ex-girlfriends not to trap him with a pregnancy. With Sabrina, he wanted nothing more than to plant his seed in her and watch it grow. There was something so exciting, so powerful in the thought that she could have a *bambino* by him, the thought suddenly overwhelmed him. He would come clean today. It was impossible to wait any longer.

Daniel pulled her tighter into him and turned them to press her against the tile wall. When her eyes met his, he saw that she knew what he was about to do. And that she couldn't wait.

"Wrap your legs around me," he heard himself say as if in a trance. His arms supported her as he lifted her to line up with his yearning erection. Her legs wrapped eagerly around him, pulling him into her center.

"*Ti amo,*" he whispered tenderly before he captured her lips with his and impaled her inch by rock hard inch.

***

The words did something to her. Even though Sabrina didn't speak Italian she'd seen enough movies to understand their meaning. It was an impossibility that Daniel loved her, yet she let herself be swept away. She didn't understand why he wasn't using protection considering that he thought her to be a professional escort. Neither did she know why she didn't stop him.

She wasn't on the pill and could easily get pregnant, but not even that thought stopped her. Suddenly she wanted nothing more than to have him inside her and have something of his, something that would still be there even if he was gone.

Sabrina tilted her hips toward him, and tightened her legs around him, forcing him to go deeper and as if he understood what she meant, he thrust deeper. His moans became uncontrolled as his body rocked inside her. His eyes were closed as he threw his head back as if to howl to the moon, his hands digging into her hips, his shaft driving into her with the force of a sledgehammer.

Pinned against the wall, she could barely move, couldn't get away from him. Not that she wanted to. Daniel filled her so completely as if he was the missing part in her life. The raw emotions she felt were new to her, new and utterly primal.

Her head spun with images of stars in the night sky, crashing ocean waves and the simple beauty of being touched by him. Her hands traveled through his wet hair and pulled him back to her face.

His eyes flew open, and she saw the signs of desire, lust and ... tenderness.

"*Per sempre,*" he whispered and pressed his lips on hers, then invaded her mouth with his tongue, and plundered her as if she were Ali Baba's cave of treasures. Never had she felt a kiss this possessive. A branding iron couldn't have said it any clearer that she was his, that he was making sure she would never want to kiss another man, never want to be touched by anybody else.

Every cell in her body filled with his essence, his scent, his energy, permanently altering her very being, awaking everything female in her and banishing the thought of anything and everything else. In his hands, she was all woman. Not a lawyer, not a daughter, not a friend. Only woman, his woman. For today, for this week.

And then he sent her over the edge and continued slicing into her as her orgasm claimed her. The tremors that shook her body were magnified by his climax, which followed hers within seconds. She felt the warm spray of his seed filling her and squeezed tightly around his cock to take everything he had to give. And wanted more.

The sound of the door bell startled her and reminded her that there was a world out there. They looked at each other.

"It's probably the housekeeper. I asked her to bring us some extra towels for the pool," Daniel mused and kissed her tenderly. "I'll be right back."

"Promise?"

He smiled. "Do you really think I can stay away from you for longer than thirty seconds?"

The door bell rang again. Sabrina kissed him, and only reluctantly, he pulled himself out of her and set her down gently.

"Thirty seconds, tops," he assured her. "God, you're beautiful!" He kissed her again.

"I'm coming," he then called out toward the door, stepped out of the shower and quickly wrapped a large towel around his lower half.

***

Damn, what a moment to get interrupted. As soon as the housekeeper was gone again, he would get right back to her and then confess everything. And it couldn't happen a minute too soon. Sabrina was ready. She trusted him. He'd seen it in her eyes.

"Mrs. Meyer, thanks—" Daniel's voice got stuck in his throat as soon as he swung the door to the cottage open and saw the person who'd rung the bell.

Fuck!

If he'd thought Audrey showing up at his hotel had been bad, he didn't really know what he should call this. Hell?

Hot and bothered in a business suit, there he stood, firmly holding onto a large legal file, about to try the ringer again.

"Ah, Mr. Sinclair, so sorry to disturb you on a Sunday morning. Jon

Hannigan, from Brand, Freeman & Merriweather."

Daniel hadn't needed the introduction. How could he forget the bastard, who was harassing Sabrina? He'd recognize him anywhere.

"Yes?" He made no move to invite Hannigan in but rather blocked the door.

"We were unable to reach you. Not a great area for cell phones up here in Sonoma." Hannigan attempted small talk.

Daniel made no comment. Should he beat him up now or later? His visitor seemed to feel the uncomfortable silence.

"Mr. Merriweather has sent me to get an urgent signature from you. The contingency bond? He said he'd mentioned it to you."

"Yes," Daniel barked back. "Where do I sign?"

"I should go over the document with you. That's why Mr. Merriweather didn't send it by courier." He tried to take a step forward, but Daniel didn't yield from his spot at the door.

"That won't be necessary. Pen?"

Nervously, the lawyer reached into his suit to find a pen, tapped on both sides of his inside pockets but came up empty. "So sorry. I must have misplaced it. You wouldn't have one?"

Daniel's anger level was at boiling point already. "Wait here."

He stalked back the two steps it took to get into the kitchen and pulled out a couple of drawers before he found a pen.

"Daniel, do you think the housekeeper could—" Sabrina's voice came from behind and suddenly broke off.

He jerked around instantly.

"Sabrina?" Hannigan. He'd stepped into the cottage and looked straight at her as she stood in the room wrapped in a towel.

"Oh no!" Sabrina shrieked.

"What the hell?" Hannigan looked from Daniel to her and back. "You little bitch. You had to fuck our richest client, didn't you?"

Daniel instantly blocked Hannigan from approaching her. "Sabrina, go back to the bedroom. I'll deal with him."

Hannigan didn't know when to shut up. "So she *does* spread her legs—for the right price."

That's when Daniel saw red. Nobody had the right to insult her. "Get the FUCK out!" he thundered. "Get out while you can still walk!" A supersonic airplane couldn't have created any more powerful sound waves.

He rushed toward Hannigan, who instantly backed away, recognizing the raw brutality hidden beneath Daniel's words. There was a promise of violence in the air as his nostrils flared dangerously. Hannigan didn't wait to find out what Daniel was capable of and ran.

With the force of a thunderstorm Daniel slammed the door shut and turned around. Sabrina had left the kitchen.

***

Sabrina's hands shook violently as she pulled her shorts over her thighs and zipped up. The trembling wouldn't stop, but she had to get the t-shirt over her head. It didn't matter that her hair was still wet. She had to get out of here.

Daniel had called her *Sabrina*. He knew her name, he knew who she was! There'd been no surprise when Hannigan had called out her name.

"Sabrina," she heard Daniel's voice as he rushed into the bedroom.

She quickly smoothed her t-shirt down.

"We need to talk."

Now he wanted to talk? Good grief, the man had timing. She searched for her handbag.

"What are you doing?" His voice sounded frantic.

"I'm leaving."

"No. Sabrina. You can't leave."

He had no right to tell her what to do or not to do. "You played me. You, you knew all along. Did you enjoy the laughs you were having behind my back? Did you?" Her voice was shrill.

"I never played you. Please. I was going to talk to you today."

She gave him a sarcastic look. "Sure you were." Talk about what, that he'd found her out? That he'd decided to toy with her, see how far she'd go? "How? How did you know?"

She realized now that *he* was the rich East Coast client the entire office had been talking about. That's why Hannigan was here, not because he'd stalked *her*, but because he was looking for Daniel. Was that how he'd figured it out? He'd seen her in the office?

"Your friend, Holly."

"Holly?"

"She confessed when I made the booking for this weekend."

It was as stab that hit her hard. Her best friend had betrayed her.

How could she? They'd grown up together, they'd looked out for each other. "I have no friend."

"Sabrina, just listen. What did you expect me to do? You pretended to be an escort, and I went along with it. I never meant to hurt you. I want to be with you. We have something special between us. I love you."

She ignored the three words she would have loved to believe. How could he love her? "I was your whore! You paid for my services, and I gave you what you paid for."

"I never treated you like that. You know that as well as I do."

"Go ahead, say it. I was your whore. That's all I was. That's all I can give you." Because if she gave him anything more, he'd just hurt her even more. Already, she'd given more than she'd ever given a man. And the feelings he'd awakened within her, he'd crushed later. His Italian sweet-talking in bed was part of the entire show. And she'd been so stupid to fall for it all, while all the while he'd lied to her.

"That's not true. Look at me! That's not true. You've given me so much more. We've given each other so much. You can't deny what's happened to us, please tell me you feel it too. I know you do. Sabrina." Daniel moved toward her, stretching his arms out, but she stepped back.

"Don't touch me!" Sabrina knew if he put his hands on her and pressed her against his half-naked body, she'd lose all her senses and give in to him.

She had to stop this now and for good. Nothing could come of this. How could he ever respect her, knowing what she'd done, that she'd slept with him for money? Like a common prostitute. He'd wake up tomorrow when his lust for her had died down and would come to his senses. But she wasn't going to stick around to see the contempt in his eyes.

"You had your fun. Quit while you're ahead. It will make a great story to tell your buddies back home. If you didn't get your money's worth I'll reimburse you."

"Why are you turning this into something sleazy? What are you afraid of?"

Sabrina shot him a hunted look. She was afraid of her heart being broken. "Consider the booking cancelled."

"The hell I will! Sabrina, you belong to me."

She stared at him. "No. I don't belong to you. I never will. Hannigan was right. Even I spread my legs for the right price. And you can't pay my price, not anymore." Her price was his love and respect, something he could never give her. What man would ever respect a woman who'd done what she'd done? She was better off cutting her losses now.

Sabrina snatched her handbag and ran for the door.

"Sabrina," Daniel yelled after her. "This is not over. You hear me?"

It was over. All she'd hurt was his pride. But her own pain went deeper. She'd fallen in love with the man who'd slept with her thinking she was a prostitute. He could have no real feelings for her. She'd only been a shiny new toy for him, something different. Something to amuse himself with. Tomorrow, he'd realize it and be grateful she gave him a way out.

Chapter Twelve

The vintner's daughter had taken pity on Sabrina and offered her a ride back to San Francisco. Sabrina had been too much of a mess to refuse the kind offer.

She slammed the door to her flat shut behind her, the noise alerting Holly to her premature return. Seconds later, she appeared from the kitchen.

"What are you doing home so early?" Holly greeted her with a truly surprised look.

"I'm not talking to you!" Sabrina snapped and headed for her room.

Holly visibly flinched. "What happened?"

She turned in the door. "Why don't you tell me since you know everything else?"

"Sabrina, please—"

She interrupted her. "Don't! I don't want to listen to any more lies today. I've had enough already. I wouldn't have expected this from you of all people. To betray me like this. How could you tell him? I hate you!"

She entered her room and closed the door behind her. Now she didn't even have anybody whose shoulder she could cry on. To know that her best friend had betrayed her was more than she could bear.

On the drive down from Sonoma, she'd already cried more than her fair share of tears. She wouldn't shed another tear, not for him and not for her best friend either.

She opened the door again and stormed into the kitchen. As soon as she opened the freezer, she realized that except for a half-eaten bag of waffles, it was empty.

"Where the hell is my ice cream?" she yelled furiously. Holly made the smart decision not to reply to her.

Sabrina needed her comfort food, and she needed it now before she went into major meltdown. She knew she was holding on by a mere thread. Grabbing a twenty dollar note from her purse, she ran for the door. She could make it down to the corner store and back. Just a few more minutes.

After running down the stairs, she yanked the building door open and froze. She hadn't expected him to come after her, not this fast anyway.

"Sabrina." Daniel's voice was soft and pleading. His hair was windswept. He'd obviously not bothered drying it before he'd jumped into the car to follow her.

"Leave me alone."

She knew that her face was tearstained and tried to turn away from him. But he was faster and took her by the shoulders before she could escape.

"I'm sorry, baby. I wasn't out to hurt you. Come back to me. I need you."

Sabrina struggled to shake off his hands, but he didn't release her. "Let me go."

"I'm sorry, I should have told you earlier, but I was so afraid you'd run away without giving me a chance. Sabrina, I'm in love with you, and I know you feel something for me too."

She looked straight into his face and suddenly knew how she could get rid of him. She'd have to lie, but what difference would one more lie make?

"I feel nothing for you. This was all about sex for me." She noticed his facial expression harden. "All I wanted was an adventure, and you provided it. I never put my heart in it."

When she felt his grip loosen and his hands fall off her shoulders, she knew he'd gotten the message. She was free. He wouldn't pursue her any longer.

"If that's what it was ..." He seemed cold now, unapproachable.

"Yes, that's what it was," she confirmed. Two seconds later, she slipped back into the building and shut the heavy door behind her. But she couldn't make it past the first flight of stairs before she collapsed, sobbing uncontrollably.

In a few months, he'd be all but a distant memory. She'd have to put this behind her. Even though he'd said that he loved her, she knew it wasn't true.

***

The next day, Sabrina called in sick. A day later, she still couldn't face seeing anybody and stayed home again.

When the door bell rang in the afternoon, she was still in her bathrobe. Holly was out.

"Who is it?" she cautiously answered the intercom. If it was Daniel, she wouldn't open.

"Courier with a letter for a Ms. Sabrina Parker. I need a signature."

She buzzed him up, and a few moments later, the bicycle messenger was at her door. She signed for the envelope and went back inside.

The return address showed a stamp from her firm. Her heart sank into her gut. A hand delivered letter from an employer was never a good sign.

Her hands trembled as she opened it.

... regret to inform you that your employment has been terminated effective ...

She couldn't read any further. They'd fired her. Just like that. And they could do it. Her employment was *at will*. And besides, she was still within her six months probationary period. They didn't even have to give her a reason. And they hadn't. Which was smart on their part. Without knowing why, she couldn't fight it.

She sank onto the couch. This couldn't be happening.

***

Daniel stomped into the lobby of Brand, Freeman & Merriweather. The receptionist greeted him instantly.

"Mr. Sinclair, good afternoon." She looked at her calendar in front of her. "I don't see your appointment here. Is Mr. Merriweather expecting you?"

He shook his head. He wasn't here to see his attorney. For the last three days he'd been brooding over Sabrina's words. His mood had gone from bad to worse, and he'd cancelled all his business meetings, not giving a royal damn if the whole deal fell apart because of it.

It had taken him three days to come to the conclusion that she'd lied when she'd told him that she had no feelings for him. After analyzing and re-analyzing what had happened the night in the cottage, when he'd kissed away her tears after they'd made love, he was almost certain that she'd lied.

But what had brought the absolute confirmation was Tim's unexpected confession over lunch today. The revelation that he and the real Holly were good friends, and that they had wanted to set him and Sabrina up on a blind date, came as an absolute surprise to him. And then he'd told him how Sabrina had cried on Holly's shoulder when she'd thought that he was still with Audrey. Proof positive that she had feelings for him.

Sabrina was a lousy liar. She'd had her heart in it from the beginning; he realized that now. She would have never agreed to the second evening and the weekend if she hadn't already started feeling something for him.

And then there was something else. When they'd been in the cottage together he'd seen the few toiletry items she'd brought, and nowhere had he seen any oral contraceptives. He was pretty certain that she wasn't on the pill, yet she'd let him be inside her without protection. He couldn't imagine that a woman who claimed that it was all about sex without her heart being involved would risk a pregnancy.

"I'm here to see Sabrina," Daniel announced to the receptionist.

She gave him a startled look. "Sabrina?"

"Yes."

"Mr. Sinclair." She cleared her throat and lowered her voice. "Sabrina doesn't work here anymore."

"What?"

"She was let go."

Fired! There was no doubt in his mind who was behind this decision. The bastard had fired her. Hannigan! Now he'd have that asshole.

"Where is Hannigan?" His voice had taken a sharp tone.

The receptionist gave him an astonished look but pointed at a door across the foyer. "He's in his office. I don't suppose you want me to announce you?" She had an inexplicable smirk on her face.

"That won't be necessary."

Without hesitation, Daniel crossed the foyer and headed for Hannigan's office. He didn't bother knocking and kicked the door open with one swift move.

Hannigan was on the phone, but as soon as he spotted Daniel, he jumped up from his desk, his eyes wide in shock.

"I'll call you back," he said into the phone and hastily put the receiver down. His voice was edgy, and it was clear that he knew Daniel wasn't here for a business meeting. This was personal.

"Hannigan, you little shit!" He didn't care that his voice probably carried all the way out into the foyer.

"Get out, or I'll call security," Hannigan warned.

Daniel took several more steps into the room, slow and deliberate steps toward the little weasel, who had sweat building on his forehead.

"You think I'm afraid of security?" Daniel laughed, but it wasn't a friendly laugh. "When I'm done with you, you won't need security, you'll need an ambulance."

Instinctively, Hannigan took a step back toward the window. "You wouldn't dare!"

Three more steps and Daniel was upon him. "That's for harassing Sabrina," he growled and launched his fist into his opponent's face so fast, the man had no time to even react.

Hannigan buckled under the impact and fell against the window. Daniel grabbed the lapel of his jacket and pulled him back. He wasn't done with the bastard yet.

"Come on, fight back, you little creep!"

Hannigan threw up his hands to shield his face, and Daniel landed his fist in his gut.

"And that's for firing her!"

The little shit doubled over. "Help! Somebody help me!" he screamed toward the door.

Daniel heard a noise at the door but didn't turn. Realizing that nobody was coming to his aid, Hannigan finally started defending himself and landed his fist in his attacker's face. Daniel's head snapped to the side then ricocheted back.

"Thanks!" Finally the asshole had given him a reason to beat him to pulp. It was no fun to beat a man, who didn't defend himself.

Fists went flying, landing in faces, chests and guts. Hannigan was a heavy guy, but Daniel made up for it with his agility and motivation. He was defending his woman. What stronger motivation could any man want?

Muffled voices carried from the door into the room. Several staff members had come to see what the commotion was about.

Daniel landed another hook in Hannigan's face who instantly careened to the floor. He went right after him.

"What the hell is going on here?" an authoritative voice cut through the snickering voices of the staff.

Daniel turned to see Mr. Merriweather enter. It didn't escape him that the secretaries had huge smirks on their faces. It appeared Hannigan wasn't exactly popular with the female staff.

"Jon! Mr. Sinclair! Explain yourselves!"

Expectantly, he stood near the door looking at the two opponents as they got up from the floor. Before either Hannigan or Daniel could say a word, Merriweather turned back to the employees, who were spilling into the room.

"Don't you have work to do?"

Instantly they dispersed, and Merriweather slammed the door shut behind them. "Gentlemen? What is the reason for this unseemly exhibition of testosterone?" He was still waiting for an explanation and gave both of them a stern look.

"He just attacked me!" Hannigan bit out.

Daniel threatened him with another hook. "That little shit here retaliated against Sabrina by firing her."

"Mr. Sinclair. It is hardly your concern whether we let any staff of ours go or not." Merriweather frowned.

"It is my concern. Hannigan has been harassing her ever since she started working here."

"That's not true!" Hannigan protested.

Daniel ignored him. "And when he realized that she'll never give into his advances, he decided to fire her."

"I'm the one, who makes those decisions, Mr. Sinclair. Not that it's any of your business, but Sabrina was let go because she neglected her work."

"Says who?"

"It was brought to my attention by Mr. Hannigan here. He's been supervising her work," Merriweather advised.

Daniel shot Hannigan a furious look. "Well, did Mr. Hannigan also bring to your attention that he surprised me and Sabrina during out weekend getaway in Sonoma? Did he bring it to your attention that he accused her of being a whore for sleeping with me? Did he?"

Merriweather went white. It was clear he knew none of the details.

"I didn't think so."

"Jon? Is this true?" Merriweather barked but received no answer. "Damn it, Jon. I was willing to overlook your indiscretions when it came to the secretaries, but this is going too far!"

He turned to his client. "Mr. Sinclair. We'll rectify this."

"I'm listening," Daniel said expectantly.

"Jon, pack your personal things and leave. The firm has no further use for you." Merriweather was pragmatic. It would be wiser to lose an associate, who'd become a liability to the firm rather than piss off a lucrative client.

"You're firing me? You can't do that!" Hannigan was beside himself. "That little bitch! Just because she's fucking a rich client, she's suddenly got free range and I get shafted!" His face was red like a ripe tomato.

Daniel swerved around and landed his fist in Hannigan's gut. Hannigan doubled over and fell to his knees, holding his stomach, his face twisted in pain.

"Never, do you hear me, never talk like that about the woman I love. Is that clear?"

"Jon, if you're not gone within ten minutes, I'll have security remove you from the building. Mr. Sinclair, please join me in my office."

Once in Merriweather's private office, Daniel finally relaxed. His attorney's decisive action to fire Hannigan on the spot had somewhat pacified him. He would give the firm another chance, even though he'd been ready to pull his account.

"Mr. Sinclair, let me just say on behalf of the firm that had we known about any of this, this would certainly not have happened. Please accept our apologies."

Daniel nodded and sat on the couch.

"I had of course no idea, that you and Sabrina ..., well I'd been under the impression that you'd been referred to us by another client not by Sabrina," he angled for more information as he continued to stand.

"You weren't misinformed. I was referred to you by another client." Daniel left it at that.

"We'll of course reinstate her, since it now is obvious that Mr. Hannigan has given me inaccurate information as to her work. I shouldn't have relied on his information alone and investigated for myself, but the circumstances ... In any case, I'll send a personal message to her right away, together with the firm's apologies." His statement bordered on groveling.

Daniel motioned him to sit, and he complied.

"I had something else in mind. I would like you to draft an employment contract for her," Daniel started.

"Of course. Certainly. We can use our standard contract and make any changes you suggest." He seemed eager to please.

Daniel shook his head. "I'm not talking about an employment contract between her and your firm, but between her and me."

Merriweather looked stunned as he tried to process his client's words. "You want to hire Sabrina?"

His expression went from surprise to disbelief and then to shock as Daniel laid out the terms he wanted incorporated in the contract.

"You can't possibly think that Sabrina would sign such a contract." Merriweather swallowed.

"I know exactly what she'll do when she reads it," Daniel responded. He hoped he was right. For once he trusted his gut. He hoped he wasn't wrong this time.

Chapter Thirteen

The week was almost over, and Sabrina had been busy updating her resume and sending it out to several employment agencies. The outlook wasn't rosy. There were specific times during the year when law offices hired, and she'd just missed the most important hiring period by a few weeks.

She'd gained at least two pounds in the five days she'd been at home by scarfing down pints of ice cream whenever she was depressed and feeling sorry for herself—which was daily.

The only good thing that had happened during the week was that she and Holly had made up after Holly had told her the whole truth.

"Tim and I only meant well. We thought you guys were so suited for each other. Tim told me so much about Daniel that I was absolutely sure this would work. We should have just waited for a better time and had some casual dinner just the four of us. It was a stupid idea. I'm so sorry." Holly's look was sincere.

"It doesn't matter anymore. It's over and there's nothing I can do to change that." Sabrina tried to sound indifferent. "He hasn't made any attempt to contact me after I told him that I don't want to see him anymore. I said things that I can't take back now. He probably despises me."

"You have his number. Why don't you call him?"

She shook her head. "It won't do any good. He wouldn't believe me if I told him what I really felt. Not now." She'd felt the ice storm surrounding him when she'd told him that she had no feelings for him. He'd never believe her now. She'd rejected him, and even if she hadn't hurt his heart, she'd hurt his pride.

***

The call from the office came Friday morning.

"Sabrina, it's Caroline." She was surprised to hear the receptionist's voice. Even through Caroline and she were friendly in the office, they weren't friends, and there was no reason she would call her at home now that she didn't work there anymore.

"Hi."

"Hannigan got fired," Caroline announced.

Sabrina's jaw dropped. "How did that happen?"

"Mr. Merriweather found out that Hannigan has been harassing you and that he fabricated things about your work not being adequate. So he fired him on the spot. That's why I'm calling. Mr. Merriweather wants to talk to you this afternoon."

She couldn't believe this. They'd fired Hannigan after he'd been so sure the partners would never touch him. She felt a huge burden lifted off her shoulders. There was some justice in the world after all.

"You mean, he might re-hire me?"

"He just said to call you and ask you to come in at three. But I'm pretty sure that's what it is. What else would he want to talk to you about, right?" Caroline asked.

"I'll be there. Thanks so much!"

***

Sabrina dressed in her best business suit and made sure she looked every bit the professional she was. If they'd offer her her old job back, she wanted to look the part. She double-and-triple-checked her outfit in the mirror. Her skirt stopped just short of her knees, and she'd opted not to wear pantyhose since her legs were tanned enough to keep them bare.

She had the need to be taller today, to feel more imposing, so she decided on her stilettos instead of the more comfortable slingbacks she normally wore. She was dressed to kill, and she would. If they wanted her back, then she wanted an apology first and foremost and then an assurance that she wouldn't be relegated to routine cases as she'd been when she'd been assigned to work with Hannigan.

A last look into the mirror, a deep breath and she knew she couldn't stall any longer if she didn't want to be fashionably late.

Her hands felt clammy when she entered the firm's foyer, and she forced a smile when Caroline greeted her.

"Mr. Merriweather is expecting you in his office. Go right in." She pressed the intercom. "Sabrina is here."

Forcing one foot in front of the next, Sabrina headed for Merriweather's office. By the time she reached it, all her hesitation was gone. She knocked and heard his voice asking her to enter.

By the time she opened the door and stepped inside, Merriweather had already rounded his desk. With an outstretched hand, he walked toward her.

"Sabrina, I am so glad you came. Please take a seat."

"Thank you." Sabrina was surprised at how overly courteous he was. It wasn't like him.

She took a seat in front of his desk, and he sat back behind it.

"Let me just say, the firm and I deeply apologize for how you've been treated. There's no excuse for it. We were aware that Jon has had … let's say, issues with female staff, but we never dreamed that he would go as far as harassing you. Hmm, we are extremely sorry that you felt you couldn't talk to us about this." He gave her a sincere look. "We … no, I hope that you know we value you highly, and we would of course offer you your job back …"

Would? What was he saying? He'd just called her in to apologize but that was it? He had no intention of offering her a job. How hypocritical was that?

"But you won't? You know what Hannigan did, but you won't give me my job back?" Her voice was flat, showing no emotions. She wouldn't give him the satisfaction that she was disappointed.

"We would be delighted to have you back, of course, but a client has asked us to be represented to obtain your …" He cleared his throat. "… hmm, services. I drafted the contract myself, and I know that our firm could never offer you what he's willing to pay."

Sabrina was more than surprised. She'd had very little client contact during her time at the firm, and it was impossible that a client had noticed her and decided to offer her a job.

"I don't understand."

Merriweather pushed a dossier across the table. "This is the contract. Before you read it, let me assure you that I've done everything in my power to protect you with the terms of this contract. It's watertight, and should you decide to accept it, believe me if I say, nobody will think the worse of you. It's an offer not many in your position would reject. We all have our price," he added cryptically.

She raised an eyebrow but didn't answer.

"And should you decide to reject my client's offer, I'll be the first to welcome you back into the firm." He stood and rounded the desk. "I'll leave you to read over the contract."

"Thank you, Mr. Merriweather."

He shook her hand and went for the door. When she heard it open and then close a few moments later, she reached for the dossier and opened it.

***

Daniel watched Sabrina sit with her back to him. He'd silently slipped into the office when Merriweather had exited, just as they'd agreed beforehand. Sabrina hadn't noticed him come in, and he remained standing motionless near the door.

As she scanned the first page of the contract, he let his eyes glide over her. He'd missed her, truly missed her and didn't know how much longer he could bear the separation.

"Oh my God!" she exclaimed as she went further and further down the page. He wanted her to have a chance to read the entire three-page contract, as impatient as he felt.

As she went to the second page, she suddenly jumped up from her chair. "Oh God!" came another incredulous exclamation. The shock at his proposal was evident, even though he couldn't see her face. It was killing him, since her expressions didn't tell him whether she was inclined to accept or reject. He needed to know. He couldn't stand the suspense any longer.

"Sabrina."

With a low shriek that got stuck in her throat, she twirled around. The sheets of paper landed on the floor, involuntarily released by her trembling hands. She was more beautiful that he'd ever seen her.

"You ..." Her voice was shaky and broke off.

He took two steps toward her when he saw her steady herself against the desk behind her and stopped. He didn't want to scare her.

"This is what you want?" She pointed at the contract at her feet.

Daniel nodded. "Yes."

"Why?"

"Because at this point I'll take whatever I can get."

He came closer and bent to pick up the pages, pressing them back into her hands. Being this close to her after not seeing her in five days, made him want to reach out and touch her.

Her eyes locked with his. "You want me to be your escort?"

"That's what you wanted, isn't it? Just sex. You said so yourself."

Sabrina held the pages up with her hand. "This is not just about sex." She pointed at a spot on the page. "Paragraph nine: Children. Care to explain what this paragraph is doing in this contract?"

"Any children resulting from this contract shall be my legal heirs," he recited a portion of the contract. "So, it's all about sex. I guarantee you'll become pregnant when you share my bed every night."

"Paragraph six: Living Arrangements. The employee will live with the employer, sharing his bed," she read.

"You know as well as I do what happens when we share a bed. Do you want me to remind you?" He inched closer to her, and he noticed her hold her breath.

"Paragraph seventeen: Compensation," Daniel stated.

"I haven't read that far," she said hastily.

"Let me paraphrase. The employee is entitled to half the net worth of the employer."

Sabrina gasped in shock. "You can't be serious."

He nodded slowly. "Read for yourself."

She searched for the place on the page and found it. Her eyes danced over the page like a ping pong ball at a competition until her mouth fell open then quickly closed again. Instead of looking back at him, she continued reading.

"I need a moment," she requested.

He stepped out of her way, moving away from her enticing scent. Sabrina rounded the desk and sat down in Merriweather's chair.

Several minutes ticked by as she read the contract to the end. He still didn't know any more than when he'd entered the office. Was she going to reject him outright? Was she going to toy with him?

When she finally looked up, her face was unreadable.

"Let me clarify this. You want to hire me as your escort, to share your bed and your home, to live with you, to travel with you, to attend every family function with you. I'm to be exclusively yours, no other lovers. And you won't have any other lovers either. Any children I might bear will be recognized as your legal heirs and will grow up as your children. In exchange I'll be entitled to half your wealth. And then the termination clause." She paused. "You should fire Merriweather as your attorney. I don't think he has your best interest in mind. The termination clause doesn't give you an out."

"That's how it's meant to be. No out for me. I'm not looking for an out, I'm looking for an in. It'll all be in your hands, just like you wanted it all along. You call the shots when it comes to termination of the contract. I'm ready whenever you are."

Sabrina shook her head. "I hope you don't mind if I make changes to this contract? Nobody ever signs a contract the way it's presented, least of all a lawyer."

She didn't wait for his approval but started making annotations. Did this mean she was willing to accept this crazy proposal? Would she really do it? He knew he wanted her to be his forever, and while he would have rather asked her to marry him, he was willing to start with what he thought she'd be more comfortable with.

She'd said it bluntly at the cottage. She couldn't be more than his whore. Fine, he'd take her and then show her what she really was: the woman he loved.

When Daniel saw her sign the contract, his heart was beating up into his throat. She was his.

"Here. I've accepted. You need to initial Paragraph seventeen. I've made changes."

Paragraph seventeen? He frantically tried to recall what the paragraph was about, when it hit him: compensation.

She nodded when she saw the realization on his face. "It's not nearly enough for what you want. I need more."

More? His heart sank. Sabrina was taking him to her cleaners. He couldn't have misjudged her like this. She'd never shown any interest in his money, but now that she had him where she wanted him, had her true side come out? God, he hoped not.

She shoved the contract into his direction. "Don't you want to read it?"

He felt as if his legs were filled with lead when he took a step toward the desk. Had she played him like a fiddle, pushed all his buttons, intoxicated him and then hung him out to dry?

"Daniel, read it," she urged him. The way she said his name made him look at her and connect with her eyes. There was nothing cold in her eyes. Instead, they were full of warmth. Her actions didn't compute with the way she looked at him.

She lowered her eyes toward the contract, begging him again to read the change she'd made. He finally did. What he saw made his heart jump. She'd crossed out the entire paragraph and written in the margin. There it was in blue ink: *Compensation – Daniel will give Sabrina his love and respect, every day, every night.*

That's all she wanted, nothing else. She'd signed the contract. He had to contain himself.

"May I borrow your pen?" Daniel was choked up as he reached for her pen.

A second later, the ink on the paper dried, his signature next to hers.

***

She looked at him and smiled. When she'd read the first few paragraphs of the contract, she'd thought he'd gone crazy. She'd even felt slightly insulted about what he was offering her, but when she'd read the termination clause, she'd realized what he was truly offering her was himself.

There was no way for him to terminate their contract. And the only way out for her? Marrying him. He would only release her from the contract if she agreed to become his wife. She understood now.

With steady steps, she walked toward him, stopping only inches away from him. She felt the heat from his body ignite the air between them.

"So you think you can pay my price?" she asked.

"I don't think so. I know so. Want a taste of it?" His look was searing, adding to the scorching heat in the room.

She licked her lips to cool them as she watched his mouth come closer. "I need more than a taste," she mumbled before his lips met hers.

His arm went around her waist as he pulled her into the curve of his body, crushing her breasts against his chest. With his other hand, he caressed the nape of her neck, angling her head to allow for a deeper kiss.

Her lips parted with a deep sigh and invited him in. He explored the deep caverns of her mouth, dueling with her waiting tongue. Everything in his kiss screamed of passion, love, and possession.

Her hands tugged on his shirt to pull it out of his pants. She needed to feel his skin. As soon as she slid her hands underneath his shirt, he moaned.

"Sabrina, I missed you. No more separations, not for a single night."

His eyes locked with hers.

"I signed the contract, didn't I?"

Daniel smiled. "Yes, you did."

"How did you know I would accept?"

"I didn't. Frankly, at some point I thought you'd throw the contract at me and tell me to get lost."

She raised her eyebrows. "And then?"

"I would have gone to plan B."

"What's plan B?"

He smirked and shook his head. "Since you've accepted plan A, I guess you'll never find out."

"I suppose I'll just have to make the most out of plan A then." She laughed and removed her hand from his chest only to place it onto the familiar bulge of his pants. Sabrina could clearly feel the heat underneath her hand.

"What are you doing?" Daniel asked slowly.

"Collecting on paragraph eleven."

"Paragraph eleven?" he asked and moaned when she stroked his growing erection through the fabric.

"Daniel, do you even know what's in the contract?"

"Remind me since my body is busy with other things right now."

She laughed. "Paragraph eleven, and I paraphrase: the employer is required to sexually satisfy the employee at all times."

"At all times?"

She nodded. "At all times. And I believe that includes now."

"Here?" He gazed around the office.

"Here. Now." She felt for the desk behind her. "Feels pretty sturdy to me," she commented on Merriweather's desk.

"Good thing Merriweather is neat and keeps his desk uncluttered," Daniel responded with a sparkle in his eyes as he hitched up her tight skirt. "How about you lose those panties?"

"I don't remember getting my other ones back from you."

"I'm starting a collection. Care to make a contribution?"

Sabrina stepped out of her panties and handed them to him.

"What do I get in return?"

He lifted her onto the desk and spread her legs as he stepped into her center and held her close. "You choose." His voice was low, and she felt his breath on her face as his lips descended on hers for a tender kiss.

Slowly, her hands went to his pants, first opening the button then pulling down the zipper. She heard his appreciative sigh when she pushed them over his hips and let them fall to the floor. As soon as she'd done the same to his boxers, her hand reached for his erection which jutted out proudly.

"Perfect," she admired him and stroked her soft hand over his shaft.

"It's been so long, baby." His eyes looked at her with unconcealed desire. Just the way she loved it. Pulling him closer by his shirt, she brought him flush against her body, his erection nudging at her warm and moist entrance.

"I want you, Daniel, all of you." She was full of the love she couldn't speak of yet. She couldn't say the words yet, but she knew he would wait until she was ready. In the meantime she'd be his escort, exclusively his.

"Please take me," she begged him and pressed her lips on his, kissing him passionately.

Sabrina let out a deep moan when she felt the head of his cock breach the tight entrance to her core. Seconds later, Daniel severed his lips from hers and looked into the depths of her eyes.

"Now you belong to me, and I belong to you. *Per sempre.*"

And then he sliced into her, ramming his eight inches of hard flesh into her wet and warm center, claiming her as she claimed him.

EPILOGUE

Three months later

Sabrina was seated at the table on the terrace of the Sinclair's home in the Hamptons. It was set for breakfast for four, but only Daniel's mother, Raffaela, was with her. She looked out over the property to the tennis court, where James Sinclair played with his son.

"When are you going to make an honest man out of my son?" She still had a slight Italian accent even after having lived in the country for over thirty years.

Sabrina turned her head away from the game and looked at the woman, who'd given birth to the man she loved.

"When it's time," she replied cryptically.

"What's stopping you? You know he loves you, and I can see you love him."

"I just have to find the courage to ask him."

Raffaela gave her a puzzled look. "To ask him? You mean he hasn't proposed to you yet? I thought I'd raised him better than that. He's even told his father that he'll marry you."

Sabrina shook her head. "And he will. But he needs me to come to him. It's what we agreed, that I would tell him when I was ready."

Raffaela raised an eyebrow and shook her head. "Modern, young people. Well, it'd better be before you give birth to my grandchild."

Sabrina stared at the older woman in surprise. Her pregnancy wasn't showing yet, and she'd barely had any morning sickness except for one or two occasions, which she thought she'd hidden well. "How did you know?"

She gave her a knowing smile. "*Cara,* you might be able to hide your condition from Danny for a little while longer, but I can tell. Or does he know?"

Sabrina instinctively placed a hand on her belly, where his child was growing, and it filled her with a warm feeling.

"I haven't told Daniel yet."

"Not told me what yet?" Daniel's voice came from the steps leading up to the terrace.

He and his father walked onto the terrace, both dressed in white tennis shorts and shirts. His father was an older version of Daniel except for the fact that he had light brown hair rather than the raven hair Daniel had inherited from his mother.

"Did your son beat you, *Caro*?" Raffaela asked her husband.

The older man shook his head and laughed. "Danny's been too busy with other things to keep up his game. Piece of cake for me." He kissed his wife.

His son didn't seem to care that he'd lost. Instead, he approached Sabrina and kissed her.

"Haven't told me what yet?" Daniel repeated.

* * *

He looked into Sabrina's eyes and saw a sparkle in them. God, the way he loved this woman. Each day, his heart seemed to grow so he could love her even more.

"I want to terminate our contract as per the termination clause."

There was a split-second of shock rocketing through his body until he realized what this meant. He pulled her out of her chair and into his arms, pressing her against him.

His parents looked at them puzzled.

"Contract?" his father asked.

Daniel smiled, but didn't take his eyes off her. "I'll explain later, Dad. In the meantime, Mamma has a wedding to plan."

He kissed her again as he heard his mother let out a barrage of exited Italian words.

"And make it very soon, Mamma, because I'm not sure what kind of selection of bridal dresses they have at a maternity store." A broad grin swept over his face when he saw Sabrina's surprise.

"You knew?"

He laughed out loud. "Baby, I've had you in my arms every night for the last three months. Don't you think I would have noticed if you'd had a period during that time?"

"And you didn't say anything?"

He caressed her with his eyes. "I knew you'd come to me when you were ready, my beautiful escort and soon my wife."

"*Per sempre,*" she answered, surprising him with the same Italian words he'd said to her for the first time in the shower at the cottage and many times after that.

"Forever," he translated. "*Ti amo*," he whispered, his breath kissing her lips.

He lifted her into his arms.

"Excuse us if we don't join you for breakfast, but I have to go make love to my bride now."

Sabrina blushed at his frank confession to his parents. Their laughter followed them and only subsided once they were inside the house and in Daniel's bedroom, which they'd shared for the week they'd been at the house.

"I can't believe you said that!" she exclaimed.

He laughed. "It's payback time for all those years I had to listen to them."

THE END

ABOUT THE AUTHOR

Tina Folsom is a member of the Romance Writers of America and writes predominantly paranormal and erotic romance. She lives in Northern California with her husband where she enjoys great food, changeable weather, and tolerates the occasional earthquake.

Her ideas for her books come from her many different careers—CPA/Accountant, Real Estate Broker, Chef, Secretary, Au-pair amongst others—as well as the many different countries she's lived in, and the people she's met over the years. And the vampires? Well, chalk them up to her active imagination.

For more about Tina Folsom:

www.tinawritesromance.com
http://authortinafolsom.blogspot.com
http://www.facebook.com/AuthorTinaFolsom
Twitter: @Tina_Folsom
Email: tina@tinawritesromance.com

16794418R00087

Made in the USA
Lexington, KY
12 August 2012